PEACEMAKER LEGACY

PEACEMAKER LEGACY

•

Clifford Blair

AVALON BOOKS
NEW YORK

PRINTED IN THE UNITED STATES OF AMERICA
ON ACID-FREE PAPER
BY HADDON CRAFTSMEN, BLOOMSBURG, PENNSYLVANIA

This book is dedicated to the memory of its author,

CLIFFORD J. BLAIR

Loving husband, father, grandfather, friend,
attorney, and writer.
He will be sorely missed by all who loved him—
family, friends, business associates . . .
and the characters who came into being in his
heart and mind to live in the pages of
his twenty-four published novels.

Prologue

James Stark knew that in order to bring in his man, he just might have to kill him.

All too often that was part and parcel of the manhunter's trade, but thankfully he'd never grown to like it. Rather, he often felt a gnawing resentment for those lost souls who forced his hand when brought to bay, or who wanted to earn a rep by downing a top gunhand like himself.

Shrugging off such futile distractions, he sat his big sorrel stallion and surveyed the settlement before him. The trail had led him here, and he wasn't surprised.

Ingalls was a two-bit prairie town situated at the edge of the Creek Nation, far from any rail lines or major roads. Guthrie, the cosmopolitan capital of Oklahoma Territory, lay a world away some thirty-five miles to the southwest.

He'd halted in a grove of cottonwoods on the outskirts

of town. From there he could see the old Trilby Saloon and
a couple more of its sorry ilk. A pair of restaurants, a blacksmith, a cotton gin, and a few other businesses, along with
a smattering of houses, made up the rest of the town. The
only two-story structure was the notorious O.K. Hotel,
owned by Mary Pierce. Nearby was the house where Sadie
Comley, the so-called Belle of of the Cimmaron, offered
girls and gambling for entertainment.

As a haven for a wanted man, Ingalls was just what the
doctor ordered. There was no law enforcement. Outlaw Bill
Doolin headquartered his gang in a cave not too far distant.
When his boys were in town they ruled the roost, often
boarding at the hotel. It was there Stark expected to find
his prey. Cass Brin would be looking for just such a den
to hole up in.

Stark felt his face tighten into a familiar grim mask. He
urged Red forward. A rangy mutt gave a lazy bark, but
other than that, there was no activity at this afternoon hour.
The air was cool, and the leaves would be turning before
too long, but the sun still struck at his eyes beneath the
brim of his Stetson. Stepping out of the sunlight into the
dimmer interior of the hotel would put him at a disadvan-
tage.

Automatically he dropped his calloused palm to brush
the butt of the unadorned Colt .45 Peacemaker riding at his
hip. He'd have to rely on it. The heavy charges of the
Winchester lever-action shotgun sheathed on his saddle
would do too much damage in close confines where innocent folk were likely to be in range. And the lethal-caliber
Sporting Rifle, with its long barrel and three-quarter mile

and above reach, would be too awkward to handle indoors. That left the .45, the Marlin .38 double-action revolver at the small of his back, and, in a pinch, the big fighting bowie in its scabbard on his gunbelt.

He hoped they would be enough. He hoped Cass Brin was still riding the lone wolf trail, and hadn't gotten hitched up with any gun-toting pards at the hotel.

He reined up before the ramshackle frame structure. For some fool reason that had always escaped him, the only entry to the second floor was a rickety ladder propped under a window. With a touch of bootheel and reins, Stark put Red next to it. Reaching out with one long arm, he shifted the ladder so it was out of reach of the window. One less escape route to worry about, he mused, unless some lame-brained yahoo wanted to see how hard the ground was.

Stepping out of the saddle, he approached the door. He squeezed his eyes shut and went through the door, opening them again as he did so. His vision adjusted immediately to the murky haze of dust and tobacco smoke.

A baker's dozen or so of hombres lounged about the lobby area which had been converted to a shabby saloon. Most of the patrons were at the scattered, flimsy tables, turning cards or lifting shot glasses, or doing both. A handful of serious drinkers lined the bar. It was nothing more than boards nailed to barrels. The barkeep was Mary Pierce herself. She looked as hard-bitten as any of her customers.

Without thinking about it, acting out of instinct long ingrained, Stark sidestepped from in front of the door as he pulled it closed in his wake. Several heads turned to appraise him. A shifting of feet and a sullen muttering showed that at least a few of their owners had recognized him.

Cass Brin was one of them. He rotated stiffly away from the bar, and the dusty light from a long-unwashed window showed the mingling of fear and anger that twisted his bearded features. He was midsized, and his threadbare shirt was stretched taut by his belly. The disreputable Stetson he wore was tilted back far enough to show a good expanse of balding skull with twisty worms of hair plastered to it by sweat.

His pistol was slung low, and the holster was tied securely around his thigh. His sorry looks aside, Brin was rumored to be a fair-to-middling gunhand.

Casually Stark moved toward the bar. He appeared to pay no undue attention to Brin, or any other man in the room. If he could get close enough, he might avoid gunplay. There was always the chance of some of these hombres siding Brin if the chips were down.

Maybe toting the shotgun would've been a good idea after all. . . .

He was still ten feet distant when Brin spoke. His hand hovered over his gunbutt. "Hold it, Peacemaker. You looking for me?"

Stark knew he'd gotten as close as he was going to get without forcing the issue. He stopped and eyed Brin up and down. "You got any objection to riding back to Guthrie with me?" he drawled.

Folks shifted away from Brin. None of them seemed disposed to side him after all. But they were mighty interested in getting to see the show.

"I ain't going nowhere with you, Stark!" Brin blustered.

"Could be you're right, Cass," Stark allowed. "But I wouldn't go betting overmuch on it."

"What beef you got with me?"

"It's the Bankers Association that has the beef," Stark explained. "You should've stopped short of gunning down that teller in the bank at Stillwater. I'm on retainer with the banks, and they offered an extra bonus for bringing you in. Just doing my job," he added wryly. "No hard feelings."

"The devil there's no hard fellings!" Brin rasped, then raised his voice. "You fellows just going to stand there and let this happen? He might be coming after you next!"

"If he was, would you back any of us, Cass?" a voice sneered. "Not likely, I'd say!"

There was some ugly laughter.

"You got no friends and no place to run," Stark told him. "Make it easy on us both. I don't hanker to kill you, and you're a mite too good for me to risk winging you."

For a moment he could tell Brin was on the edge of backing down, and he felt a faint sense of relief. Maybe he could avoid another notch on his soul.

Then the taunting voice of the heckler rose again. "Go ahead, Brin, crawl on your belly for us! Show us what a yellow-bellied snake looks like!"

"Hang you, Sab Tucker!" Brin spat over his shoulder, and Stark saw that his moment of weakness—or good sense—was past. No chance now Brin was going to come quietly.

Beyond Brin he could see the sneering features of the bank robber's nemesis. Sab Tucker was a bulky hombre sporting a black longhorn mustache on a face that might've been handsome save for a sallow slackness of features.

Stark knew his sorry breed—a barroom bully, given to picking on those who weren't in a position to fight back. Straight up, Stark doubted Tucker would ever have the guts to face Brin.

Tucker tipped his head back and opened his mouth again.

"Ride clear, tinhorn!" Stark grated in cold, seething anger.

Tucker's sagging jaw jerked shut.

"Forget him, Brin," Stark urged.

"You ain't taking me in, Peacemaker." Brin was bristling like a riled catamount.

"Yeah," Stark said, "I am." Now that the moment was here, a surging wildness coursed in his blood.

Brin made a savage, wordless sound and his hand snapped for his gun. Stark gauged his speed and made his own draw with a flicker of his hand. The .45 Peacemaker came level and stabbed flame. Its thunder reverberated in the room and made the dust ripple in the air.

Brin took two stumbling steps back and buckled in the middle. As he fell Stark eyed the rest of the crowd through the haze of powdersmoke. None of them moved.

After a moment he nodded at a fellow near the front of the group. "Check him for me," he requested easily.

A pair of seconds went by, and then the cowpoke obliged. "He's dead, sure enough," he reported, kneeling by Stark's victim.

Sure enough, Stark thought grimly. The wildness was

fading from his system to be replaced by a bleak bitterness. He holstered his gun.

"Winner buys drinks; rules of the house," Mary Pierce raised her voice from behind the bar.

Stark glanced at her and nodded. "Keno." It was a good way to quell any hard feelings in the crowd.

While they bellied up to the bar, Stark crossed to look down at Brin. The man had been a blamed fool, he mused. He'd let himself be goaded into dying.

"Real fast shooting." Tucker might've been an evil spirit summoned by Stark's conscience. "But I know someone a long sight faster."

Stark lifted his eyes to the big man. "Stow it," he suggested. "I ain't Brin."

Tucker took a step back, raising his hands defensively. "Hey, don't get me wrong. I ain't calling your hand; just passing the word so you'll know to be on the lookout."

"Not interested," Stark drawled dissmissively.

"Figured you'd want to know," Tucker persisted. "I've seen him draw, and now I've seen you, and I got to say he's got a leg up on you." His voice was loud enough to carry, and some heads turned at the bar. "Yessir, sure would've turned out different if you'd been facing off with my pard."

"Is that a fact?" Almost against his will Stark let himself be drawn out. He was close to wishing Tucker would start something just so he could have the pleasure of shutting the blowhard up. You couldn't shoot a man—even wing him—for being a pest, no matter how tempting the notion.

But Tucker just wasn't going to quit until he'd had his say. "Your pard got a name?" Stark's voice was tired.

"He does, but he don't use it much. He goes by the Sooner Kid."

"Another kid?" Stark said laconically. "The brush is full of them these days."

"Not like him, they ain't," Tucker asserted.

"I done heard of this Sooner Kid," one of the bystanders spoke up. "Supposed to have a draw like a greased rattlesnake."

Stark had heard of him too, but he didn't want to feed the fire by admitting it. The Kid had been cutting a swathe up in the Unassigned Lands where no legal authority held sway.

His moniker was an odd one. The Sooners were the unscrupulous and illicit settlers who had crossed the boundary line and staked their claims before the starting gun for the 1889 Land Run that had opened Oklahoma Territory for settlement. If the Kid had been one of that sorry bunch, it didn't speak too highly of him.

"Land thief, was he?" Stark said aloud.

Tucker wagged his head back and forth. "Not a bit of it. His family owns a passel of land hereabouts. One day he'll inherit it. He came by his name because he always gets his gun out sooner than the other fellow! I seen him in over a dozen showdowns now, and he always comes out the winner. Took down one of your compadres not long ago, Peacemaker. Another bounty hunter went looking for him on some trumped-up charge. Now that guy's pushing up daisies."

"Never been fond of flowers myself," Stark gritted darkly. "Sure not enough to become fertilizer for 'em. Much rather see garbage like the Sooner Kid filling that role."

The snickers from the bystanders told Stark his dark humor had been well received.

"Laugh all you want now," Tucker snarled. "But if you ever come up against the Kid, he'll wipe that smile offa your face in a hurry. I tell you, he's the fastest gun to come along in a coon's age."

"I'm shaking in my boots," Stark shot back.

"You're sure making him nervous, all right, Tucker," one of the onlookers took up the ribbing. "I can see his trigger finger twitching from here."

Tucker blanched visibly at the pointed reminder that he was goading a man not known for his patience. Stark was grateful for the comment coming from someone other than himself. He hoped Tucker would be shamed into silence, but no such luck. The man's whiskey-sodden brain wasn't given over to sound thinking in this instance, Stark noted ruefully.

Tucker raised his hands defensively again. "Like I said, I'm just trying to pass on some information you might need down the road, Peacemaker. Forewarned is forearmed, ain't that what they say? No call to get your back up at me."

Tucker's attempt at appeasement didn't at all ring true to Stark, but he let it ride. Besides, the blowhard Tucker had a point. With his rep, and the trade he followed, there was always the chance he and the Kid might get crossways

Clifford Blair

down the road, and it never hurt to know something about your enemies, no matter how questionable the source.

But the pointlessness of Brin's death, and the role Tucker had played in it, left Stark with a bad taste for the whole affair. He'd face up to the Sooner Kid when and where he had to, if ever their showdown chanced to come about.

Still, it wouldn't do to let any of the onlookers get the notion he was leery of going up against a yahoo the caliber of the Sooner Kid. "You just tell Sooner, or whatever he calls himself," he advised Tucker, "that if he ever tries me, he'll be looking up at dirt a whole lot sooner than he would otherwise. Now, get out of my way, or you'll be doing it even quicker than that!"

There were some rough guffaws at Tucker's expense. He glared at Stark. "Just remember, Peacemaker, every dog has his day."

"Reckon that would include you," Stark said dryly.

A commotion outside the building turned heads. There was a startled, fearful cry that stretched out then ended in a clearly audible thump. Following came a broadside of outraged and pained curses.

Stark could've reached the door first, but he went with the general exodus and held back to let a couple of the more curious blunder out ahead of him. No gunshots met them, so Stark elbowed his way through the press and stepped into the open. Unholstered, his fisted gun dangled alongside his leg.

A disheveled figure floundering around like a hooked fish was the center of attention. The onlookers parted to make way for Stark. The hapless fellow on the ground stared up at him.

"Hang you, Stark!" he panted. "I busted my ankle on account of you. I thought you were on your way up to get me next!"

"So you jumped out of the window?" Stark cast a disbelieving glance up at the aperture. The ladder still stood where he'd moved it just out of reach of the window.

He looked back at the would-be escape artist. "Shoot, Ned, you ain't bad enough or worth enough for me to waste my time tracking you down!"

Ned Cooper was a drifter and sometime sneak thief whose path Stark had crossed once or twice. He had no idea what secret trespass of Ned's might have given him the notion that Stark was on his trail, and, he decided, he didn't really want to know at this point.

"Blast it, Stark, it's all your fault I got my leg busted up!" Ned was still grousing.

Stark opened his mouth to deny the charge, then realized how foolish the whole exchange was, and didn't bother. Instead he dug left-handed in his jeans and came up with a coin. He thumbed it so it spun high in the air then dropped to the dust beside Ned.

"There," Stark told him. "That should cover whatever treatment you can get in this flea-bitten town. Pray I don't ever come after you for real."

Wearily he turned toward the hotel. He wasn't eager for a ride back to Guthrie with Cass Brin's silent company. The whole affair had turned into a dark comic opera, he mused, with Brin as a tragic villian, and Tucker typecast as the court fool.

Stark didn't feel much like the hero of the piece. He was disgusted, but as much with himself as any other character involved. Because, as much as he knew about the evils of the sin of pride, and as much as he disliked the need for killing, it still rankled to have Tucker boast that a second-rate outlaw like the Sooner Kid could beat him to the draw. He almost hoped he'd have the chance to prove Tucker wrong.

If he *was* wrong. . . .

Chapter One

"Jim," Prudence McKay asked, "have you ever heard of a gunman known as the Sooner Kid?"

She was strolling beside him on the sidewalk, a shawl around her shoulders and a hand resting almost possessively on his crooked arm. She gazed up at him expectantly. "Why are you scowling?"

Not for the first time, Stark wished that she wasn't so blamed perceptive when it came to reading his moods. "Yeah, I've heard of him. A month or so back some yahoo told me the Sooner Kid would beat me hands down if I ever faced off against him."

"Is that true? Could he beat you?" Her voice carried a surprising amount of interest in the subject.

"How would I know?" Stark retorted sharply. "I've never

even seen him, much less hauled iron against him. Why? Do you think he could beat me too?"

"Don't be ridiculous!" she snapped in answer. "I wouldn't dare venture an opinion in such a matter. I was merely reacting to your obvious concern."

Remotely Stark knew how childish he had let the exchange become. Thankfully they were not on one of Guthrie's main thoroughfares, with their bustling noonday traffic of horse-drawn vehicles, riders, and pedestrians. The cobblestone street they had taken on their route back from lunch was relatively empty of other folks.

Not that it would've been the first time they'd had a difference of opinion in the public eye. On the best of days in their relationship sudden squalls could develop as fast as a twister blowing in across the Oklahoma prairie.

"Is this what's been bothering you for the past few weeks?" Prudence demanded now, like she was cross-examining a witness on the stand.

"Nothing's been bothering me!" Stark denied.

"That's not true," she persisted. "You've been surly and on edge ever since you brought in that bank robber. I thought it was because you'd had to kill the man. I know that always disturbs you—even when it can't be helped."

Hearing the concern and understanding in her voice, Stark got a rein on his temper. As usual she was right. "It was that and more," he allowed. "That killing could've been avoided except for one thing—or one person, I should say. Reckon I really let Sab Tucker get under my skin, and that rankles a bit."

"Sab Tucker? Who is he?"

Tersely he sketched the events at the disreputable hotel in Ingalls. He rarely spoke with Prudence of the details of his work, and generally she wasn't wont to press him. She'd always had trouble accepting his violent profession. It was just one of the things that kept them sparring on the edge of an uneasy sort of friendship.

"I'm surprised you've let something like that bother you," she commented archly when he was finished. "You told me once you don't have anything to prove. And this Tucker doesn't seem worth fretting about. Let it go. There's nothing you can do to change the past anyway."

Right again, Stark had to admit. He'd come to realize lately just how much he valued her approval, and she was certainly demonstrating a lot of support and acceptance he hadn't expected. At times in the past his prowess with a gun had proved low on the list of things she found admirable about him.

A rare smile pulled at the corners of his mouth. "I guess what you're saying is true," he said dismissively. "I'll probably never even cross paths with the Sooner Kid anyway."

Prudence's tone changed subtly. "I wouldn't be so sure. If you did, would you pick a fight with him?"

"Not unless I had to in order to protect myself or someone else." Stark was growing suspicious of her motives. "Now, what's all this about? Is the Kid your client or something?"

"No," she answered quite seriously. "But I have some clients who might need protection from him."

"Who might they be?"

"His mother and sister."

Stark frowned slightly. "What happened? Did the kid's father die?"

Prudence blinked. "How could you know that?"

"Something Tucker said." They'd reached the neat frame one-story building with *PRUDENCE McKAY, ATTORNEY AND COUNSELOR AT LAW* stenciled on the frosted glass door. "Here's your office. Why don't you tell me about it?"

She flashed a quick smile. "Oh, I'm so glad you're interested!" Then a look of concern replaced the smile. "But you're not just—"

"I already told you I ain't looking for a fight with the Sooner Kid or anybody else." This time Stark read her mind. He hoped the statement was the truth.

But Prudence appeared to take his words at face value. "Sarah and Donna Dunsmore, my clients, have an appointment scheduled for an hour from now. If you'd like, you can meet them then."

"Unless I'm too frightened of the Kid," Stark said dryly.

Prudence wrinkled her nose fetchingly at him, and ushered him into her comfortably furnished office. Martha, her motherly secretary, served them tea in the informal seating arrangement snuggled in one corner of the room. She closed the door behind her as she left.

Although he'd worked with Prudence before on bodyguard jobs, Stark still sometimes found it hard to believe that this vivacious and stunningly attractive brunet was known as one of the savviest and most successful attorneys in Oklahoma Territory. Prudence McKay, Attorney and Counselor at Law, was quite a woman to boot, Stark thought.

He watched her remove the prim hat and shawl and hang them on the rack in the corner. Even the stiff, high-necked dress couldn't completely conceal the lovely, womanly figure underneath. Stark caught his breath as she turned to him with another provocatiove smile. *Yes, quite a woman,* he again acknowledged silently to himself.

It took an effort to get his thoughts back on the matter at hand. "So the Sooner Kid is the black sheep of the clan," he surmised once they were seated, their legs almost, but not quite, touching. With the pretense of shifting to a more comfortable position, Stark put more space between them. This was a business meeting after all, he reminded himself.

"He might better be described as the prodigal son who never repented," Prudence responded. "I believe a little family background is in order. First, to be technically accurate, I should've said that Sarah and Donna are his stepmother and half-sister. The Kid's father, Clarence Dunsmore, died in an unfortunate gunfight a little over two weeks ago."

"And the Kid smells an inheritance."

Prudence nodded. "Dunsmore Senior had quite a name for himself in Texas as a young man. He worked as a hired gun and may have even ridden the outlaw trail. The Kid, whose real name, incidentally, is Blake Dunsmore, was a result of his father's younger days. His mother was a saloon girl, and Dunsmore left her in a family way. Blake grew up wild and mean." Prudence's full lips thinned in disapproval at the whole mess.

"Eventually Dunsmore got a bounty on him, and left Texas, and Blake, behind him—not that he'd ever had much to do with the boy as a youngster. In Kansas, Dunsmore settled down and seemingly did his best to mend his ways. He married a decent God-fearing girl, Sarah, who was several years his junior. He made some efforts then to locate his son, but was unable to do so."

Unwillingly Stark felt a faint edge of—not sympathy, but maybe understanding—for the Kid. Every man lived and died by his own choices. But for some, the wrong choices were made easier by their kinfolk and their upbringing.

"Dunsmore did well in Kansas as a businessman, but when Oklahoma Territory was opened, he couldn't resist returning to the frontier. He sent his daughter, Donna, back East to school, and he and Sarah came to the Territory on the heels of the Run. He bought up enough sections from dissatisfied settlers to establish a small cattle empire."

"Enter the Sooner Kid, I'd bet," Stark predicted.

"Exactly. He showed up with a pair of hardcases and succeeded only in antagonizing his father, who threw them all off the ranch."

"I'll lay odds one of his hardcase pals was Sab Tucker."

"At any rate, there were hard words exchanged between father and son. They almost came to blows from what I'm told."

"And he got himself disinherited."

Pruddence nodded affirmatively. "Dunsmore left a hand-written will that acknowledges the Kid as his son, but bequeaths everything equally to his wife and daughter. They retained me to handle the probate."

"Has the Kid stuck his nose into things?"

"He showed up unexpectedly for the funeral, then rode out, promising he'd be back for his share of the estate."

"Does he know Dunsmore cut him out of the will?"

"His stepmother told him as much. He called her a name I won't repeat, said something worse about his half-sister, and swore he'd break the will."

"Can he do it?"

Prudence frowned. "Clarence did a good enough job for a layman, I suppose. His will meets all the requirements of a holographic will. It's entirely in his handwriting, and signed and dated by him. It names Sarah and Donna as co-executors. He even had it witnessed."

"Sounds secure enough. But you don't need me to help out with a will contest. You must expect the Kid to do more than hire some shyster to represent him in the probate."

"I could be wrong, but I'd rather not take any chances. He might attempt to terrorize them into granting him a share. And if both of the legatees die, then the Kid becomes the sole heir. I'm not sure I'd put plotting such a thing past him, and my clients, for their part, believe they have reason to be concerned."

Stark wasn't prone to dispute her reasoning or the fears of her clients. "Where will the trial be held?"

Prudence scowled darkly. "In Pottawatomie County."

Stark cocked an eyebrow. "Before the Shotgun Judge?" he inquired laconically.

"That's right." Prudence's pretty features looked as though they'd been darkened by a storm cloud. "Judge Horatio Hatch himself. Do you know him?"

"I watched him hold court once in a case where I was involved. He kept a sawed-off double-barrel Greener on the bench and used its butt as a gavel. I kept expecting it to go off and blow a hole in the ceiling. He didn't have much trouble keeping order."

"He's a barbarian and a lame excuse for a jurist!" Prudence declared hotly. "Heaven knows how he was able to get appointed as federal judge for that or any other county. The man's a disgrace to the legal profession."

"What happened?" Stark asked slyly. "Did he rule against you in a case?"

Prudence gave her head a liberated toss. "As a matter of fact, he ruled in my favor. But that doesn't mean I approve of his serving on the bench. He doesn't even hold court in the county seat. He prefers that pagan whistle-stop town of Earlsboro, because that's where he lives. Which, I must say, is appropriate!"

"Whiskey town," Stark muttered. He had to agree Earlsboro wasn't much of a place to have a federal court.

Abruptly Prudence glanced at the fine Gilbert clock on the mantel. Rising, she crossed to her desk and began arranging papers stacked atop it.

"I've already filed the petition to probate the will," she spoke as she worked. "The hearing is in one week."

"Did you give notice to the Kid?"

Prudence nodded grimly. "As required by law. We published a notice and mailed a copy to his last known mailing address. Presumably he received it, or has learned of it by word of mouth." She grimaced. "There's nothing like inviting the enemy into court and letting them take their best shot at you. Sometimes the probate laws go a little too far in protecting disinherited heirs, if you ask me."

"We can be sure the Kid knows all about the hearing, then," Stark concluded. "He may hire himself a lawyer, or he may simply take matters into his own hands and try to make himself the sole surviving heir."

"Or he may do both," Prudence added. "I've asked Sarah and Donna to come here today so I can go over what they can expect at the hearing."

"Are they traveling alone?" Stark asked sharply.

"No, they'll have William Fuller, Donna's fiancé from back East, traveling with them."

"Some tenderfoot riding shotgun?" Stark queried, then caught the hint of a smile from her. He cocked his head expectantly.

"You may have a higher opinion of his abilities than you do of most greenhorns," Prudence advised. "You may even like him. He's a New York City police officer."

"I know of one Eastern law officer who has done pretty well at surviving out here, but Oklahoma Territory ain't New York," Stark growled.

"Which is why I'd like to have the estate hire you as bodyguard. And I did ask Marshal Nix to send a deputy to accompany them to Guthrie."

As usual Prudence had a good grip on the reins of her case. "Okay," he accepted aloud. "I'll ride herd on mom and daughter and Eastern beau. On one condition."

Now it was Prudence who cocked her head expectantly. She was almost smiling again. "Let's hear it."

"That I'm in charge when it comes to matters of their safety. Or yours, for that matter."

"Why, that goes without saying, of course," Prudence assured him demurely.

"I'd feel better if it was said."

"You're in charge of our safety, and I'm in charge of all legal matters," Prucence stated contritely. "Satisfied?"

"And I make the decisions about dealing with the Sooner Kid."

"Agreed, so long as you don't pick a fight with him."

"It's a deal. I won't tangle with him unless I have to, so long as I'm on the payroll."

They eyed each other warily.

The two of them did work well together, Stark reflected, except when they were butting heads or feuding in what sometimes seemed frighteningly close to lovers' spats.

He often thought of her as a wild mare, never broken to halter, who might not ever gentle down. Of course, the unsettling notion followed that even the wildest horse, once it got used to the halter, could eventually learn to like it. He wondered whether that applied to Prudence or to him.

Moving suddenly away from her desk, Prudence crossed to a small decorative mirror mounted on the wall, and checked her appearance. Stark had the sense that it was an automatic, almost unconscious part of her preparations for meeting with clients. She might nearly have forgotten his presence.

He suppressed a grin. "Relax," he drawled. "You look lovely as always."

She had her hair done up primly, and he had the satisfaction of seeing the back of her pale neck, above the white collar of her dress, flush a fiery apple red.

"Blarney," she retorted over her shoulder, then turned gracefully away from the mirror. "But thank you nonetheless, sir." She executed a flawless curtsey.

"Just telling the plain truth, Miss," Stark rejoined. But somehow, as his eyes met hers, his tone missed the humorous note he'd tried for. Of a sudden, although she was a room away, he felt the unnerving impact of her feminine nearness.

Prudence must've felt something of the same thing. She gave a little gasp, and the color drained from her face like a plug had been pulled. Stark swore the temperature in the room shot up. His legs flexed and he found himself on his feet. Prudence looked breathless and expectant.

A single knock sounded on the door. "Miss McKay?" came Martha's precise tones.

Prudence tore her eyes away with a visible effort, and tried to speak. On her second effort her voice was reasonably level. "Yes, Martha?"

The secretary opened the door. For a moment she stood frozen, as though the surging emotions in the room had fled past her in escaping.

"Your clients are here, ma'am," she managed then.

Prudence's sigh seemed to mingle relief and regret. It echoed Stark's own exhaled breath.

"Please show them in, Martha."

Chapter Two

The handshake of New York City Constable William Fuller was firm, and his palm was harder than what Stark expected. The Easterner was of medium height, with a sturdy build and clean features beneath sandy hair. He had, Stark was pleased to see, made some effort to lose the greenhorn look. Still, he seemed a mite uncomfortable in new boots and denims.

There was one item that was unchanged. A regulation black leather police belt encircled his lean waist. But the cutaway holster where he packed his sidearm was anything but regulation. It was designed for the type of fast draw that sometimes meant the difference between life and death in the back alleys and dark byways of any Eastern metropolis.

"James Stark." Fuller's brow furrowed. "Formerly of the Pinkertons, correct?"

"A few years back," Stark affirmed.

The younger man grinned slightly. "Even in the Police Academy they still talk about the undercover work you did when the Department and the Pinkertons cooperated in closing down the Tenth Avenue Gang and their hijackings on the Hudson River Railroad."

"I wasn't alone," Stark demurred.

"You were when you went undercover. How long was it that you stayed under?"

Stark felt Prudence's inquiring gaze. "Too long," he answered tersely. Then, to change the subject, he added, "What precincts have you worked?"

"The Second and the Twenty-First."

Stark nodded. The Second Precinct was known for its bloody street riots; the Twenty-First was infamous for its violent youth gangs. Fuller had walked some tough beats. His eyes dropped to Fuller's holstered pistol. It looked to be one of the six-shot .32 Colt new police double-action revolvers manufactured especially for the New York Department.

Before he could comment, the delicate clearing of Prudence's throat let him know she'd heard enough about law enforcement back East. Stark held his tongue and let her direct the trio to chairs.

He was the last to be seated. Settling back against the yielding upholstery, he listened silently as Prudence explained probate procedures in the Territory. For the most part they'd been lifted whole hog from the statutes of nearby states, and were nothing if not cumbersome and time-consuming. He wondered if lawyers a century hence would still be burdened by the same bulky system.

With hooded eyes he studied the three guests. He'd liked the cut of Fuller, and as he gauged the womenfolk he felt a gut anger for the Sooner Kid replacing any softer feelings he'd had earlier. It took a sorry specimen to set about aggravating such females as these, especially when they were kin.

Sarah Dunsmore was a small woman with prim features that carried her age well. Stark read in her calm voice and restrained attitude the kind of determination and character that went with being the helpmeet of a repentant hardcase turned successful businessman and rancher. He suspected Sarah herself had played no small part in her man's reformation.

A good woman could do that, he mused, and he resisted the urge to glance at Prudence. Instead he eyed the offspring of Sarah and her reformed hardcase.

Donna Dunsmore was a younger version of her mother, lovely in her youth and her obvious affection for her beau. Eastern schooling had given her appealing social graces. But Stark sensed the rancher's cowgirl daughter was not too far beneath her sophisticated manners. He could well see why young William Fuller had fallen for her looks, her spirit, and her beguiling contrasts.

"Tell me about your husband's last meeting with his son," Stark requested when Prudence had finished her explanation of the legal matters.

With only a trace of huskiness to mark her feelings, Sarah repeated with more detail the story Prudence had related of the Kid's visit to the ranch which had ended in the falling-out between father and son.

"Clarence was heartbroken about it all," she finished. "He wanted to make amends, but it was clear Blake would never be satisfied no matter what he was offered. Later, Clarence told both Donna and me to never, under any circumstances, let ourselves be caught alone with him."

"He didn't need to tell me that," Donna spoke up with a boldness probably bred of her Eastern sophistication. "I didn't care for the way he looked at me." She shivered visibly and no longer appeared quite so sophisticated. "And I'm his *sister*."

"I hope he does show his sneaking face around here," her fiancé interjected tautly. His hand dropped to the holstered police revolver.

Stark eyed him. His regard for the younger man slipped a notch. "Don't stay on the prod," he advised coolly. "The Kid isn't some dime-novel villain, or some Tenth Avenue Gang thug."

Fuller's features hardened. "The West isn't the only place they teach a man how to shoot fast and accurately," he declared.

"No, but it's a good place for a greenhorn to bite off more than he can chew," Stark said bluntly.

A spark flashed in Fuller's blue eyes, and he looked like he was about to respond. Then Donna, beside him, leaned slightly so her shoulder brushed his. At the contact he set his jaw and his retort remained unspoken.

He grunted acknowledgement of Stark's words. "I'm afraid I'm not too professional where Donna's safety is involved," he confessed ruefully.

Stark didn't look at Prudence. "That's when it's most important to be be professional. Don't go trying to give the Sooner Kid or anybody else out here an even break. Situations where a fast draw decides the issue come along often enough without looking for them." Stark ignored what he fancied was a disdainful sniff from Prudence, as though to remind him that he didn't always follow his own advice. "Besides," he added aloud, "I plan to be riding point if we run into the Kid or any of his pards."

"Hopefully a confrontation won't be necessary," Prudence said pointedly.

Stark knew it was time to switch trails. "When did your husband write his will?" he asked.

"Over a year ago," Sarah recalled. "He'd been to Guthrie on business and was returning that evening when something spooked his horse, and it threw him. He told me later he'd been almost dozing in the saddle. He was banged up some, but I think his pride was injured more than anything.

"His horse was too well-trained to go very far. He caught it and went on, but he said getting thrown like that made him start thinking that he ought to get his affairs in order.

"There was a roadhouse not too far along, and he stopped, got some paper, and wrote up the will right then and there. He had three other customers at the roadhouse to witness it. He spent the rest of the night there and came home in the morning. He was still concerned enough that he had the doctor in Shawnee give him a checkup just to be safe."

"Where was the roadhouse?" Stark wanted to know.

"East of here; it's called Rowland's."

"I've heard of it," Stark said tonelessly. "Do you know if he was acquainted with any of these witnesses?"

"No, they were all strangers to him."

Stark resisted the impulse to shake his head in discouragement. They had a will drawn up in a notorious hardcase den, by a man who'd just gotten thrown off his horse, with three patrons of the place as witnesses, and a disinherited gunslinger son as the centerpiece of the document. It was a sorry kettle of fish. Rowland's Roadhouse was about the last place in the territory to look for upstanding witnesses.

He didn't voice his thoughts, though he could tell Prudence realized he was troubled. "How was your husband killed?" he continued his questioning.

Sarah swallowed, then set her jaw resolutely. "It happened in Shawnee almost by accident. He ran into a man who remembered him from his old days, before he'd gotten himself straightened out.

"This stranger bore some kind of grudge against him, apparently. Things took place very quickly, and the witnesses couldn't make sense out of all that was said. Then the man pulled his gun and started shooting. Clarence got off one shot as he fell. They both died right there on the street where it took place." She broke off and bowed her head quickly. Her daughter slipped a consoling arm around her shoulders.

"Sorry," Stark murmured. Then he addressed Prudence. "Any connection between the gunman and the Kid?"

"None that I've been able to find."

The old longrider's past had finally caught up with him, Stark reflected. He wondered what pieces of his own earlier years would cross his trail someday.

"I'd like to go over what takes place when a will is contested," Prudence said, taking charge of the meeting.

Stark glanced at Fuller. "Let's you and me go do something about that peashooter you're carrying."

"My revolver?" Fuller frowned, but followed suit as Stark rose. "What's wrong with it?"

"Double-action .32, isn't it?" Stark queried instead of answering.

"That's right." Fuller's hand dropped possessively to the butt of his holstered weapon.

"Out here most hombres favor something with a little more punch to it. You don't want to have to use two shots to stop some yahoo who can stop you with one." He shepherded Fuller into the outer office.

"James." Prudence's voice caught him as he made to follow Fuller out into the hallway. He turned with a pretty good hunch what was coming.

Prudence drew him back into the outer officer out of earshot of the younger man. "What are you doing?" she demanded in a whisper, confirming his hunch with her first words. "A moment ago you were urging him to stay out of trouble. Now you're all but encouraging him to go looking for it. Why are you doing this?"

"Because if I don't do it, he's liable to get his head

blown off by some gunslick with a slower draw but a bigger gun."

"That reasoning doesn't hold up!" she scoffed. "How do you even know he has a fast draw? How do you know he can draw a gun at all?"

"By his equipment—by the areas of New York City where he's worked. This is my territory you're meddling in now! I know my business. By this time you should know enough to trust my judgment on issues like this. Fuller's gonna be siding me in this fracas, and I want him as prepared as he can be. His life—all our lives, for that matter—might depend on how he handles himself in a showdown. Having a heavier weapon might just give him the edge he needs!"

Prudence sniffed disdainfully. "Or it might just get him killed! You saw how anxious he was to confront the Sooner Kid."

"I'll work on his attitude, too. He's a good man with good instincts. He'll soon learn not to take on more than he can handle."

"Don't be so sure. Donna might not always be there to settle him down like she did here in the office."

So Prudence had also picked up on Donna's role in calming Fuller's outburst. Her observation skills irritated Stark all the more. "Look," he gritted, "the man deserves even odds. That goes without saying before good judgment and self-control and all the things you're concerned about ever enter the picture. Now I'm gonna do my best to see that he has those even odds—and that includes getting him a weapon with more firepower!"

Prudence glowered up at him. "Suit yourself! But what if having a bigger gun just makes him want to prove himself all the more?" Wheeling with a swirl of dress and petticoats, she marched back into her office.

Stark glowered some himself at the doorway where she'd disappeared. Then he rejoined Fuller in the hallway. The Easterner eyed his stony features speculatively, but didn't speak as Stark pushed open the outer door.

"Gunsmith is this way," Stark directed. Fuller matched the brisk stride he set down the street.

Stark nodded at the cutaway holster on the police belt. "That ain't regulation," he drawled, needing confirmation of his earlier guesswork.

"No, it's not. I don't wear it with dress uniform, but a few of us in the ranks favor holsters like this on patrol. It gives us an advantage in pulling our guns. The sergeant winks at it."

Stark nodded, wishing Prudence had heard Fuller's words.

The gunsmith, Ned Morgan, was a tall, lean man with receding hair. " Morning, James," he greeted.

"Ned," Stark acknowledged him, and made the introductions. Then he extended his hand palm up to Fuller. "Let's see your iron."

Slowly the constable passed it over. Stark hefted the light six-shooter thoughtfully.

"A .45's kick takes some getting used to," he mused aloud. "You're already accustomed to this weight, so we need something with more power, but about the same size.

Ned, let's have a look at that Colt new service revolver."
He pointed at the display case.

The gunsmith produced the weapon. Stark weighed it in
his hand then proffered it to Fuller. He sensed the edge of
resentment in the constable as he swapped his .32 for the
more powerful revolver. No gun-toting professional liked
having unsought advice pushed on him.

Stark set the .32 on the counter as Fuller slipped the .38
experimentally in and out of his holster.

"Feel about the same?" Stark asked.

"It's close," Fuller admitted.

"Pull," Stark ordered.

Fuller flexed his arm casually. The .38 came out of the
cutaway holster with a lazy smoothness.

Stark scowled. "Again. For real this time."

Fuller met his gaze challengingly.

There was a blurred circular motion at Stark's side. For
a piece of a heartbeat the old .45 Peacemaker was out and
leveled with the hammer back. Then like a conjuring trick
it was once more in the holster with the hammer safely
down. Something less than a second had passed.

Fuller's eyes were wide.

"For real this time," Stark repeated flatly.

Fuller blinked the astonishment from his eyes. He
straightened fully erect, then made his draw. The gun came
up smooth and level once more. And he was fair middling
fast, Stark assessed. Even better, he didn't waste time and
effort dropping into a crouch before drawing.

Fuller holstered the gun and cocked his gaze inquiringly
at Stark.

"Snap it out of the holster as you pull it," Stark advised. "Put your hand, wrist, your whole arm into it."

"That isn't what you did," Fuller objected with an edge still in his tone.

"What I did takes a lot of time and practice to learn. We're building on what you have. Like this." Stark clasped the .45's butt then popped it up with a convulsive flexure of every muscle in his arm and shoulder. It was almost as fast as his other draw. "Make sure you keep your grip on the gun," he added.

A bit hesitantly, Fuller tried it. He looked surprised at the results. Again he experimented, with more assurance this time. And again.

"You're getting it," Stark praised sparsely. "You can try it with ammo out on the trail. Give us a half-dozen boxes, Ned."

While the gunsmith was complying, Stark looked again at Fuller. "That .38's a double-action like your .32, so firing it will be pretty much the same." He scooped the smaller-caliber weapon off the counter and returned it to its owner. "Tote it in your saddlebag. If you're expecting trouble, stick it in your belt as a backup."

"Sometime I'd like you to show me that other draw."

"We'll see."

Fuller accepted the answer. He turned toward the gun-smith. "What do I owe you?"

"I'll cover it," Stark cut in. "Put it on my tab, Ned."

"Now I'm twice beholden to you," Fuller commented. "First you give me a tip that could save my life, then you buy me a new gun that could do the same thing."

"Insurance. Come on, let's go."

"Wait a minute. You've got two, maybe more draws to choose from. How do you pick which one to use?"

"Depends on the man and the circumstance," Stark said.

Chapter Three

From two miles out on the prairie Stark could smell the scent of alcohol wafting on the breeze from the town of Earlsboro.

William Fuller reined up beside him with practiced ease. In his career as a beat cop, Stark had learned, the younger man had pulled a stint in the Second Precinct's First Mounted Squad. That experience showed in the skill with which he sat his saddle. The new .38 rode comfortably in his custom holster.

Fuller jerked his head back over his shoulder toward the buggy occupied by the three women. "Miss McKay has been telling me about Earlsboro," he advised. "Is it as bad as she says?"

Riding point, Stark had caught snippets of the conversation. "Probably," he admitted. "Judge Hatch mostly keeps the lid on things, but he's got a pretty loose interpretation of the law. Since we're not far from the Indian Lands, there's a lot of whiskey flowing in Earlsboro.

"By law, the Lands are dry, so there's plenty of folks who cross over to Oklahoma to do their drinking and kick up their heels. I'd guess three-quarters of the businesses in town are saloons, bawdy houses, or gambling dens. Every one of them peddles alcohol of one sort of another."

"That's all it is, a town of bars and dance halls?"

"Oh, there's a little farming community attached to it, with a blacksmith and a cotton gin, and a few other respectable establishments, but they don't amount to much." Stark paused a moment then added, "It'll be a rough crowd regardless of whether the Kid's there or not. Keep your eyes peeled, especially when it comes to looking after our ladies."

"Understood, Sergeant," Fuller said tersely, and sketched a quick salute. He let the ghost of a grin touch his lips before swinging back beside the buggy.

Stark grinned a little bit himself. The New York City police officer had shed his arrogance and combative spirit and now showed the makings of a good hand, whether it was sitting a saddle, helping with the camp chores, or practicing with his new revolver. There were worse men to ride the river with, Stark reckoned.

He hoped that Prudence had noted the fact that her fears about Fuller becoming unruly or aggressive were unfounded. The constable's assurance with the new weapon Stark had insisted upon had only served to increase a spirit of quiet cooperation.

The trip to Earlsboro had been uneventful, save for the nagging sensation of predatory eyes observing them, a sensation that had clung to Stark like a burr on the back of his neck. Twice he had made wide sweeps off the rutted trail that served as a road. And twice the watcher, if such there had been, had eluded him without leaving so much as a bent blade of buffalo grass in his wake.

Nerves, Stark told himself, but in his gut he knew better. It wasn't nerves that had kept him alive all these years riding alongside trouble. It was a hunter's instinct for when the tables were turned and he himself was being hunted.

Now as they were nearing their destination, the feeling was fading, and he forced himself to shrug off his concerns.

But he wouldn't forget them.

He spied a line of trees up ahead and knew they skirted a creek. He signaled the buggy to follow as he headed in that direction. Might as well have a bite to eat and give the women a chance to freshen up. Everyone needed to be at their best considering what they would be facing in Earlsboro.

As Fuller saw to watering the horses and the Dunsmore women broke out the rations, Prudence left them and approached Stark.

"You're worried about something, aren't you?" she asked without preamble. "I saw you veer off to check things out. Did you find anything?"

Stark shook his head. "No, I was just playing it safe. I had an uneasy feeling, that's all. Likely it was just nerves."

Prudence studied him with a raised eyebrow. "I've never known you to be nervous . . . without a good reason."

He shrugged. "There's always a first time."

She opened her mouth as if to speak, then thought better of it. Stark was glad she didn't press the matter.

He nodded toward Fuller, who was backing the buggy team back into their traces after watering them. "He's turning into a passable trail hand, isn't he?"

Prudence smiled up at him teasingly. "And I suppose you're going to gloat about his progress?"

"Who me? Gloat?" Stark bit back a smile. "Now that wouldn't be mannerly, would it?"

Prudence laughed out loud. "That's never stopped you before. Go ahead and say it. You were right. You might as well take credit on the rare occasion when that happens."

This time Stark couldn't stop the smile that split his face. Her laugh always had that effect on him, "*Rare occasion*, is it? Seems like you have a mighty selective memory, Counselor."

"Perhaps you haven't yet grasped the most basic premise of the legal profession. It's my job to select and present only those facts that move my case forward," she retorted coyly.

Stark was struck by how appealing she looked. "I guess I didn't realize that mode of thinking carried over into your personal life as well," he teased.

She sobered suddenly. "Thought patterns are ingrained. I can't help doing it—any more than you can keep your professional life from influencing your personal dealings."

Stark felt immediately saddened that the coquettish light had gone out in her eyes. He had enjoyed her standing there flirting with him. Then his heart skipped a beat as he fully acknowledged the fact of what he'd just realized. She had been openly flirting with him. That in itself was a first.

A similar realization must have stolen over Prudence as well, for she took a quick step backward away from him. "Well, I guess we both better eat something and be on our way. Earlsboro is just up ahead, right?"

"Right." Stark scowled sourly and followed her over to the buggy. He was at a complete loss as to why all of a sudden he felt so irritated with her . . . and with himself.

There wasn't much going on along Earlsboro's main street when they arrived in the early afternoon. Horses stood hipshot at the hitching rails in front of the bars and gambling halls and other dens of iniquity. A few loafers and vagrants lounged outside.

A dance-hall girl, not bothering to wear anything over her revealing costume, crossed the road in front of them. She glanced their way with hard, painted eyes. Stark spotted a man's motionless from sprawled in an alley. Drunk or dead, he calculated, and wouldn't have bet either way.

He had dropped back to ride just ahead of the buggy, and kept his eyes shifting as they passed down the street. He was in full fighting gear, with bandoliers for his long guns crisscrossing his chest. His formidable looks, and the presence of the women, turned more than a few heads.

They moved past one of the fancier saloons, and a fellow slumped on a bench with a jug for company straightened and gave the group of newcomers a long intent stare. Then, scrambling to his feet, he disappeared through the batwing doors, abandoning his jug beside the bench.

Stark cut a glance at Fuller and saw that he'd noted the

man's behavior. Prudence, handling the buggy's two-horse team, looked cool and aloof. Mother and daughter bore nearly identical expressions of steadfast determination. The widow kept her eyes straight ahead. Donna's eyes kept flitting to Fuller's dashing mounted figure.

Stark reined in at the single respectable hotel. It was the only business not selling alcohol on the whole length of Main Street. As the others halted, he swiveled around in his saddle to look back at the fancy saloon. While he watched, the batwing doors were pushed open and a trio of men, backed by a small crowd of followers, emerged into view.

Most of the crowd remained grouped in front of the door. A single buckskinned fellow detached himself and paced deliberately over to prop his shoulder against the building's wall near a towering mule. The animal was burdened by a saddle and gear. It was tethered to a tie weight apart from the horses.

The trio, moving in a close sort of triangle formation, slanted across the street toward the newcomers. Stark recognized one of the two men in the rear as the boot-licking Tucker. The other fellow, dressed like a gambler or a shyster, was a stranger to him.

"That's Blake in front," he heard Donna advise softly, but he'd already guessed that the leader of the trio was the Sooner Kid.

The unrepentant prodigal son was no youth, which, despite all he knew of his background, took Stark a little by surprise. The Kid had seen thirty years and then some. His face was ragged and unshaven. A greasy mane of shoulder-length black hair tumbled from beneath his Stetson. He was going to seed in his midriff, but he moved with the callous arrogance of a man who has learned he is good at killing and has come to enjoy it.

Some kid, Stark thought grimly.

He stepped down from Red, careful to keep the three-some in his vision. They spread out a little as they drew near.

Fuller shifted his mount a bit. Stark gave him an all but unnoticeable shake of his head. Fuller caught it. His expression didn't change, but he stayed mounted. *Yep, a good hand*, Stark had time to reflect. If it came to flying bullets with three-to-two odds, it was best to have one of the two mounted. A horse could make a mighty good weapon.

The Kid halted a dozen feet distant and his cronies followed suit. He hooked his thumbs in his gunbelt and rocked back and forth on his heels. He wore two pearl-handled guns tied down in well-oiled holsters. Stark wondered if he was fast with both hands. Most two-gun men carried the second pistol for show or for use as a backup.

It was hard to watch all three of them at once, and Stark kept most of his attention on the Kid. For the nonce the Kid ignored his kinfolk.

"I heard there was a high-dollar shootist messing in this affair." The Kid's voice was roughened by years of tobacco, dust, whiskey, and gunsmoke. "You're the Peace-maker, ain't you?"

Stark hitched his shoulders. "You're doing the talking."

The Kid snorted. "I've heard tell you ain't as big as your rep."

There was no point in trading jibes with this yahoo, Stark reminded himself. He wasn't here to goad the Kid into a fight; he had promised not to do so, in fact.

Behind the Kid, Tucker sneered at Stark.

"The Sooner Kid," Stark heard himself say scornfully. "Just another gun hound looking to earn a name from all the other 'Kids' who've come down the pike ahead of you. Only two of them ever came close to living up to their reps: William Bonney and Harry Longabaugh. Billy's dead at the hands of the law, and Sundance is running with Cassidy and will end up the same way. You couldn't hold a candle to either one of them on a still day, and nobody will remember your name or your rep an hour after you're gone."

The Kid's harsh features blanched. Though he couldn't see her, Stark was sure he felt Prudence's penetrating stare drilling into him. Not trying to pick a fight, was he? What in tarnation had gotten into him?

But it was too late to crawfish now, and he'd prodded the Kid pretty hard. A feral eagerness was in those slitted eyes, and he'd unhooked his thumbs from his tooled twin-holstered gunbelt.

The dude-looking hombre behind the Kid edged nearer and spoke low and terse so that no one else could hear him. The Kid scowled in frustration then seemed to make a major effort to regain control of himself.

After a moment he hooked his thumbs back into his gunbelt. "You'll keep, Peacemaker."

Stark made a major effort of his own and bit back a retort. His fool pride had almost put not only the women he was hired to protect, but Prudence herself, in the middle of a showdown. He ignored the mocking smile that still hung on Tucker's face.

"Howdy, sis." The Kid was looking toward the buggy. "Who's your pretty traveling companion?"

"I'm Prudence McKay, their attorney," Prudence took up the answer in a cold tone.

The Kid let out a whistle. "My shyster don't look nothing like you. Maybe you'd like to switch sides and represent me in this little hoedown. I'd sure make it worth your time. And mine as well!"

"Unlike your counsel, I exercise some discretion in the clients I choose to represent. And there's no further need for this conversation. What needs to be said can be said in court."

The Kid's chuckle was ugly. "Not everything, I reckon." He tilted his head toward the mounted Fuller. "Who's the pretty boy?"

"The name is William Fuller. I'm Miss Dunsmore's fiancé."

"Oh, a city boy from back East, by the sound of it. Nash here hailed from those parts a spell back until things got a little messy for him." He jerked his head to indicate the natty gunman who'd reined him in a few moments before. "Don't figure he'd want to use the handle he had then. Out here, he's just Nash."

"We're not interested in you or your accomplices."

"You sound almost like a law dog. But whatever you are, you got good taste. My sis is a mighty fine figure of a woman."

Fuller stiffened in the saddle. "You filthy street thug!" His fingers curled trembling over the butt of his .38.

"No!" Stark rapped sharply, but in his gut he had the burning realization that things had already gone too far. His own restraint was about to be undone by Fuller's instinctive and justifiable reactions to the Kid's words.

"Gentlemen, gentlemen, please calm yourselves," the cultured voice cut smoothly across the tension stretched taut in the street. "This is no way to resolve an issue, and the judge, while he may be lenient in many matters, takes strong exception to unauthorized multiple-party gun disputes in his streets."

The bizarre pronouncement, as soft and unyielding as velvet-covered steel, froze them all like fence posts. Then Stark edged his head around a bit, careful to keep the Kid and his cronies in the side of his vision. He saw the expected figure of a slender, almost slight black man clad in a sober broadcloth suit. His right-side coattail was flipped ominously back to bare the holstered butt of a pistol at waist height. Like a sideshow magician, he had somehow managed to appear on the boardwalk in front of the hotel. From that vantage point he commanded the entire scene.

"Howdy, Bailiff," Stark said out of the corner of his mouth.

"Mr. Stark, good to see you. And you as well, Miss McKay." His eyes barely flicked toward her as he made the acknowledgement.

"Who the devil are you?" the Kid burst out.

"Allow me to introduce Thaddeus Jenkins," Stark supplied with a wry tone of enjoyment in his voice. "He's

Judge Hatch's bailiff and sergeant-at-arms. I don't advise you to cross him."

Once more the gunman called Nash spoke a few low, urgent words to the Kid. Thaddeus looked on and smiled thinly.

The bailiff was a valuable man to have siding you in just about any type of fracas, to Stark's way of thinking. Handy with a gun as well as a law book, he'd used brains, wits, and sheer determination to study the law and earn a license to practice in the Territory, despite ugly pressures opposing him.

Stark suspected that it was the bailiff's knowledge of the law that kept the unruly judge from straying too far afield in his court procedures and rulings. In a fairer world, Thaddeus would've likely been a renowned jurist himself.

Nash had apparently offered the Kid sound advice. He gave a frustrated shake of his head. "This ain't finished," he growled. "Court or no court."

He wheeled and led his cohorts back to the saloon where they disappeared inside with the crowd of onlookers. The buckskinned hombre remained propped against the building wall near his mule, observing the goings-on.

William Fuller had relaxed a mite and was eyeing Thaddeus curiously. Stark made the introductions. As always, even when dealing with troublemakers, the bailiff was the soul of politeness.

"I've been out of town on business," he explained. "I'm glad my return coincided with your arrival. The judge does take exception to large-scale shootouts in his town under most circumstances. Now if it was only two gentlemen settling their differences at gunpoint, that would be a different matter. The judge doesn't like to interfere in minor personal disputes." Irony laced his tone.

"It doesn't sound as though His Honor has changed," Prudence observed in a similar tone.

"Oh, no ma'am, not in the least. He's certainly set in his ways."

"Like some other men I could mention." She gave Stark a barbed look that he pretended to disregard.

"The judge would appreciate the opportunity to see you and your clients in his chambers when you've had a chance to freshen up," Thaddeus continued. "I understand he has already met with Mr. Dunsmore and his legal counsel."

"There are those in the legal profession who would frown on a judge meeting separately with legal counsel for opposing parties," Prudence observed.

"Why yes, there are, Miss McKay," Thaddeus agreed with urbane courtesy.

Prudence shook her head. "How do you do it, Thaddeus?"

The bailiff gave one of the few genuine smiles Stark had ever seen from him. "You and I, Miss McKay," he said, "we both have our crosses to bear."

Stark sensed a bond of professional kinship between the two attorneys. Both had overcome prejudice and discrimination to succeed in their profession. Likewise, the heights to which either could hope to rise had definite limits.

"We'll be along to meet with His Honor presently," Prudence promised.

"I'll relay that to him, Miss McKay."

Stark stayed where he was as Prudence escorted her clients into the hotel. About to follow them, Fuller halted, eyeing Stark questioningly.

"Go with them," Stark ordered. "Keep an eye on things. I'll catch up."

Fuller hesitated, then moved to follow on the ladies' heels.

Stark waited until they all had vanished into the hostelry, then cast his gaze once more at the buskskinned form across the street.

Stepping from the boardwalk, he sauntered in that direction.

Chapter Four

The buckskinned stranger made only a single movement as Stark approached. Indolently, he bent one leg and placed his moccasined foot flat on the wall against which he leaned. It was a studied move, a fighting man's move. Like a spring, that planted foot and flexed leg could thrust their owner into action in a heartbeat's time.

In a sense Stark felt like he knew this man already. He had the cruel stamp of a hunter. In his earlier years his prey would've been buffalo, and maybe renegade Indians on behalf of the Cavalry as a scout. After that, wolves and rogue bears and cougars, and wanted men—some wanted by the law, others by enemies who were willing to put a price on their heads.

Bear traps hanging on the mule, along with a fancy repeating rifle and an ancient Sharps Big .50, confirmed

Stark's hunch. The mule itself had the rolling eyes, flattened ears, and trembling hip muscles of a man-killer. Stark gave the beast a wide berth, and the hunter grinned a tight, feral grin that lasted no more than the blink of an eye.

His buckskins were threadbare, stained and stiffened with old blood and grease. Around his lean middle a cracked and discolored leather belt was cinched tight. From it hung a skinning knife, a beat-up revolver, and a keen-edged, steel-bladed tomahawk.

Shaggy hair was pulled back in a braid that might not have been loosened in months or even years. The eyes in the grizzled face were the color of the sun-bleached prairie in the dead of summer. Years of poring over tracks and staring across vast distances had drawn those eyes into a perpetual squint.

As those tawny eyes fell on Stark he felt once again that burr of uneasiness he had known on the trail. Maybe this wasn't the first time those baleful orbs had rested on him.

"How's hunting?" he asked laconically.

"Not bad." The hunter's voice rasped as if he wasn't used to using it. "But then it ain't like the old days either."

Stark tended to agree with him. He tilted his jaw toward the bear traps on the mule. "Not many bears left in these parts."

"There's a few over to the Cross Timbers area. But I don't use them just for bears. There's plenty other game."

"One of them could break a man's leg if he stumbled into it," Stark commented.

"For a fact; seen it happen myself."

Stark indicated the repeating rifle sheathed on the saddle.

It had an oddly curved S-shaped lever. "You must plan on missing an awful lot."

"Nope; just don't plan on running dry of cartridges."

"Not likely with that. The magazine holds—what?—thirty-three shots?"

The hunter hesitated. "Yeah, that's right," he said then. "You know your guns, sure enough. There's not many that would recognize an Evans."

"Not many of them made once the company went under. Too bad; it was a good piece."

Stark wasn't just making talk. The Evans old-model sporting rifle packed a formidable load of firepower. The four-column fluted magazine in its butt held more rounds than any other rifle or handgun made. It could give its owner an overwhelming and deadly edge against any opponent.

Or any prey.

The hunter shifted his jaw as if he was chewing on something tough. "Name's Lute Talon," he volunteered.

Stark had never heard of him, which didn't have to mean he wasn't good at what he did. It could mean he just never left witnesses around to tell the tale.

"James Stark," he responded, but couldn't be sure if the name meant anything to Talon or not.

"I'll remember you," Talon promised. "Could be our trails will cross again."

"Could be," Stark agreed. Then he added dryly, "Good hunting to you."

Talon gave an amused snort.

Stark left him there. Once more he steered clear of the

wall-eyed mule. Yep, Talon was a hunter, he mused. Just what was it he was here to hunt?

Fuller was loafing outside the hotel, waiting on the ladies. Stark joined him. They were keeping a wary eye on the town when the womenfolk emerged at last.

Prudence looked askance at Stark, but offered no spoken rebuke of his earlier prodding of the Kid. "Shall we proceed?" Her tone was all business. Then her eye fell on Talon, still lurking outside the saloon. "Heavens, who is that villain?"

Stark gave a shake of his head. "Either an old lobo who's outlived his day, or one who's let himself be put on a long leash. Whichever it is, he's bad medicine. Best to ride clear of him."

"You needn't worry about that on my account," Prudence assured him.

Thaddeus Jenkins met them at the door of the converted saloon where Judge Hatch conducted his court. Stark had heard the tale of the judge closing down the saloon on some legal pretext or the other, just so he could seize it in lieu of a fine from its owner. He lived in what had been the owner's suite upstairs.

The judge himself reminded Stark of an enormous whiskey barrel to which smaller powder kegs had been attached, all hinged to supply limbs and even a bushy head.

For this informal hearing, or whatever it was, he had enthroned himself at one of several massive tables scattered about the large room. He rose to his feet like a mountain being born from the earth, and greeted his visitors in booming tones.

The sawed-off double-barrel Greener shotgun, which served as his gavel, was stuck casually under the belt encircling his tree trunk girth. The pistol grip of the weapon seemed always within reach of one ham-sized hand.

He waved them forward with gruff charm. "Have a seat, all of you. Mrs. Dunsmore, Miss Dunsmore, welcome to my court. Miss Prudence, always a pleasure. Peacemaker, good to lay eyes on you again. And you must be Constable Fuller. Pleased to have you in the Territory."

With the pleasantries out of the way, he settled back down. A file folder was in front of him. One thick forefinger flipped it open with surprising deftness. "I always like to meet folks before the trial gets started," he explained. "I run my court according to my own rules, but it's still a court of law. Thaddeus there knows the law backwards and forwards. He can cite you chapter and verse when the need arises. I respect the law—make no mistake. I'll listen to both sides of any matter, and I'll make my ruling. Need be, I'll enforce it."

He looked square at each of them before setting his gaze on Prudence. "Young lady, here's the objection that's been filed against your petition. I don't reckon as how you've had a chance to see it as yet." He passed a legal-sized sheet to her.

Stark saw that, like many legal documents, it was a standard printed form on which key details had been typed or handwritten on lines provided. He narrowed his eyes to make out the name of the lawyer who had filed it. Lance Grimes. The name didn't ring any bells.

"Now, this business of a man disinheriting his only son,

even a black sheep son, is bothersome to me," Hatch went on in his one-sided discourse. "It goes against the grain. A man shouldn't reject his own flesh and blood."

"Yet the law permits it so as the intent is stated in the will," Prudence ventured to interject.

"I'm pretty darned well aware of that!" Hatch snapped.

Prudence bobbed her head in polite acknowledgement, but was not to be put off. "Your Honor, it sounds as though you have already decided this case."

"Nope, nothing of the sort," Hatch denied promptly. "I don't decide until I hear all the evidence. A man ought to be able to leave his worldly goods to whomsoever he pleases."

"I'm pleased to hear you say that."

Hatch grunted as if her words were a vindication.

"Your Honor," Prudence persisted carefully, "I would like to make a request of the Court."

"And just what might that be?" Hatch eyed her warily.

"I request that you no longer meet with either myself of my opposing counsel unless both he and I are present."

Hatch snorted explosively and shifted his ponderous body.

"I'll meet with anybody I please, and under any circumstances I please, in running my court. You remember that, young lady!"

"I also request that you address me as 'Counselor' or 'Miss McKay' in your court." Prudence's voice had drawn tighter. "I will, of course, enter both of these requests into the record."

The judge reared back slightly. His nostrils flared above

his tangled beard. "I'll take it under advisement, *Miss Mc-Kay*."

"Thank you, Your Honor," Prudence said humbly.

Hatch shook his head ruefully. "I'd forgotten what a vixen—no offense!—you can be in a courtroom brawl. It'll be something to see you and Grimes toe the line! Looks like I'll have my hands full keeping order."

Prudence disregarded the comments. She opened her valise and withdrew a sheaf of typed pages. "I anticipated there might be a contest," she advised. "Here is my brief in support of the petition. There's also a copy for opposing counsel."

Hatch accepted the documents. "Thaddeus," he tossed over his shoulder.

The bailiff had already stepped forward. "Sir?"

"Take these. Give one to Grimes. Read the other one."

"Yes, sir."

"Now, show these folks out. This court goes into session at nine o'clock tomorrow morning," he added to his guests.

Once the bailiff had ushered them out, mother and daughter huddled for a moment with Fuller. The young constable appeared to have been pressed into early duty as the man of the family. But he seemed willing enough to accept that responsibility. At the moment he looked to be doing his best to reassure the two women.

Prudence's mouth was a thin line, as tight as the reins on a balky bronc.

"Your assessment of our case at this stage, young lady?" Stark drawled.

Her breath exploded in a strangled gasp. "Just marvelous!" she declared almost under her breath. "We've got a renegade judge who is predisposed to favor the other side, is biased against me because I'm a woman, and is looking forward to being the referee of the whole thing like it was one of your prizefights!"

"You ought to be pretty used to things like that," Stark pointed out more seriously.

"I've come to expect bias in dealing with lawyers and judges is these parts," Prudence admitted. A little of her ire was spent now. "And I know judges all too often make up their minds before they hear the evidence, but I've seldom seen one with the sheer gall to admit it ahead of time."

"Just giving you fair warning," Stark suggested.

She shook her head in disgust, then glanced past Stark, and bit back any reply she might've planned to make.

"You must be Miss McKay. I was hoping to have a chance to meet you before we argued this little case tomorrow."

The speaker was as sleek and well-fed as a yearling show steer at the county fair. He affected a fancy Eastern-style suit, with the customary derby replaced by a flat-brimmed Stetson. With a casual look he dismissed Stark from the proceedings.

"I'm Lance Grimes, Miss McKay. Or perhaps I should make it 'Prudence?' " He lifted his eyebrows inquiringly for permission.

"Of course, you'd be Lance Grimes," Prudence said in chaste tones. "And 'Miss McKay' or 'Counselor' will be just fine." She smiled as though she was granting a favor, and gripped the pale soft hand he proffered hard enough to make him blink.

He was only taken aback for a moment, however. "Very well, Counselor, I just wanted to give you an opportunity to withdraw your petition."

"Why ever on earth would I do that?"

Grimes was almost as tall as Stark. Beneath the high-dollar suit coat his shoulders were broad and well-set. He shrugged them with assumed casualness, as though he'd practiced the movement in front of a mirror. "Why, to save us all some time, and to save your clients some public embarrassment. I will have your petition thrown out, you know."

"On what grounds?" Prudence countered skeptically.

Again came the shrug. "Lack of testamentary capacity on the part of Mr. Clarence Dunsmore, of course. There's obvious evidence of his inability to know or understand the nature of the document, which he was manipulated or co-erced into signing. It would seem you'd realize it's a simple matter. I've handled many cases of this sort in the past, as I'm sure you have as well."

Prudence managed the same air of nonchalance. "It's true I've handled many cases like you described, but this clearly isn't one of them. Mr. Dunsmore wrote his will himself," she pointed out. "No one with any interest in it was present when he did so. It was duly witnessed by on-lookers with no connection to Mr. Dunsmore, as I'm sure an attorney with your experience has verified by now. So there's no possibility of alleging undue influence, even if you could make that argument successfully against a spouse or adult child."

Grimes was unperturbed. "Undue influence or not, he still lacked testamentary capacity."

"I'm assuming you believe you can prove that assertation."

"Well, of course I can prove it. That *is* the reason we're having this hearing, is it not?"

"What evidence to you plan to present?"

"You'll find out tomorrow if you persist in seeking to have that bogus will admitted."

"Oh, you'll find I'm very persistent. And don't forget— you are required by law to reveal your evidence to me prior to trial."

Grimes flashed a sardonic smile. "That might be true in other jurisdictions, but I don't think our good Judge Hatch concerns himself too much with procedural rules or details."

Prudence couldn't constrain a grimace of agreement, but she countered quickly. "Still, such procedural violations open up the avenue for my clients to appeal any irregular rulings."

"Oh, but legal appeals do move so slowly through the courts, don't they, Miss McKay? And while your clients are appealing, I believe my client would feel legally justified in moving ahead to claim any inheritance that might be granted him by this court."

Stark knew the events Grimes had just hinted at were likely to take place. The Sooner Kid wouldn't feel at all bound to wait for the outcome of a court appeal. If this case was decided in his favor, he'd move immediately against Sarah and Donna Dunsmore. And the outcome of such a confrontation wouldn't be pretty or just.

And, of course, Prudence knew that her legal skill was the only thing standing in the way of that happening. Stark saw a glint of cold resolve flash into her eyes.

"Speaking of your client, Mr. Grimes, is he going to testify?" she demanded then.

Grimes gave his theatrical shrug. "I'm not sure there will be a need for him to do so."

"Oh, there'll be a need all right, because I'm going to call him as my witness. There are certain aspects of your client's case that need to be brought out, and I don't think he'll allow you to present them. So, rest assured, he will testify."

"I can see my expectations about your legal judgment were wrong," Grimes conceded with a superior smile. "You will make an interesting opponent. In a way I'm glad you're going ahead with your case, inadequate though it may be. There's nothing like a challenge to sharpen a man's skills."

"Or a woman's."

"As you say. Until the morrow then."

Prudence watched him saunter away. Then she turned to Stark. "And *he* makes the situation just about perfect!" she said wrathfully.

Chapter Five

"Court is in session," Thaddeus Jones intoned. "The Honorable Horatio Hatch presiding. All rise."

Obediently, Prudence rose with the rest of the folk in the converted barroom. Surprisingly—or maybe not, given the near-showdown the day before—there were a number of townspeople present in the courtroom to view the trial.

Scowling as if he resented even these scant formalities, Judge Hatch lumbered to the heavy chair he had mounted on a low platform behind the bar. From this makeshift position he presided over his court.

Prudence saw Blake Dunsmore's two sidekicks among the audience, as well as Constable William Fuller. Her gaze lingered briefly on Jim Stark's alert and reassuring figure. All guns were required to be checked at the door, excepting only Thaddeus's pistol and the judge's shotgun. But she was rather dubious that Jim had, in fact, given up his entire arsenal, in particular the hideout revolver he carried. But she had weightier concerns than this on her mind just now.

Her clients were seated at the counsel table with her. They were in their Sunday finery. Both mother and daughter showed some signs of strain. That was hardly unexpected under the circumstances. Prudence was feeling a bit of the strain herself. She hoped none of it showed in her composed expression.

At the other table Lance Grimes looked as pompous and condescending as ever. From the moment she'd met him, he'd grated on her nerves. She was pleased to think that the reverse was also true.

Blake Dunsmore—probably at the insistence of his attorney—had at least made an effort at looking respectable. Mostly, she thought, he looked uncomfortable in a suit and tie. His long, scraggly hair had mostly been combed out. He did more than grate on her nerves. He made her flesh crawl as if centipedes were scurrying over her.

"Be seated," Thaddeus directed as Hatch settled into his throne.

The bailiff himself took a seat at a table facing the courtroom. From it he could keep an eye on the spectators as well as transcribe a record of the proceedings. Hatch plucked his pistol-grip shotgun from under his robes and placed it deliberately on the bar. Prudence felt a tingle of tension along her spine.

"You lawyers get up here," Hatch ordered by way of asking counsel to approach the bench.

Grimes sauntered forward empty-handed. Prudence carried a single slim file folder. She stayed far enough from Grimes so that his greater height wouldn't give the appearance of dominating her.

"Either of you got anything we need to cover before we pull the gate on this rodeo?" Hatch growled.

"Ready to proceed, Your Honor," declared Grimes.

"I have three preliminary motions to enter, Your Honor." Deftly Prudence slipped two sheets from the folder. The original she passed to the judge; a carbon went to Grimes.

"First, I'd like to ask that this proceeding be transfered to a different court on the grounds of pre-trial publicity and notoriety. Failing that, I would respectfully request that Your Honor recuse himself for the reason, as stated in chambers, that you have predetermined conclusions in this matter. Finally, if you will not accede to this request, then I move for jury trial."

Hatch snorted and looked at Grimes. "You got anything to say?"

"I have no objection to you hearing this matter, Your Honor. Quite the contrary in fact; I welcome it."

Hatch snorted again. "Denied on all counts," he told Prudence.

She had expected nothing more, but she cut a surreptitious glance at Thaddeus to be sure he was faithfully recording all this. She fancied there was a ghost of wry sympathy in the bailiff's eyes for the brief moment he met her gaze.

"Go ahead, ma'am," Hatch said gruffly.

Well, his form of address was an improvement, she supposed. "If it please the court," she began, "I have filed a holographic will in this matter. It is entirely in the decedent's handwriting, as I am prepared to prove by affidavit and testimony. Further, it is signed and dated by the testator, thereby meeting all the statutory requirements for admission. It names my client, Sarah Dunsmore, as the executrix. I request that it be admitted to probate, and that my client be sworn in as executrix pursuant to its terms."

"You got any witnesses you want me to hear?"

"At this time I am prepared to call my clients to testify."

Hatch frowned darkly. "I can pretty well guess what all they'd say. Don't reckon I need to hear it. What about you, Grimes? You got anything?"

"Your Honor—" Prudence interjected sharply, but Hatch waved her to silence with a peremptory paw.

"I do have a witness I'd like to present, Judge." Grimes was eager to snatch attention away from Prudence.

"I formally object to being prevented from presenting evidence in support of my petition," Prudence stated, just to be sure it got in the record.

"Who's this witness?" Hatch asked Grimes as though Prudence hadn't spoken.

"Dr. Daniel Kirby." Grimes turned to motion at a nondescript middle-aged man among the spectators.

"What's he got to do with this?" Hatch growled.

"He will establish that Mr. Dunsmore did not have the requisite capacity to understand the nature of his actions when he wrote the so-called will."

"I'll hear him," Hatch said without hesitation.

"I demand the right to cross-examine this witness!" Prudence snapped. The trial was rapidly becoming a farce.

"You'll get it," Hatch assured her. "But first he's got to testify. Get him up here, Grimes."

A steady determination settled over Prudence. Too much in the way of objections would only get her thrown out of this absurd court, she realized. She must bide her time.

Dr. Daniel Kirby took the stand. Even having a good idea what to expect, Prudence listened with grudging respect as Grimes made his case.

His questions were precise, and Kirby made a good witness. Yes, he had been educated in medical school back East. He had come West for his health. He had spent fifteen years practicing in cowtowns, boomtowns, and frontier villages. He had examined and treated hundreds, perhaps thousands, of injuries common to the frontier, ranging from snakebites, to gunshot wounds, to broken limbs and other injuries resulting from throws or falls from a horse. That definitely included head injuries. Yes, he had had many an occasion to observe the effects of head injuries resulting from mishaps involving horses. Finally, he had studied the circumstances surrounding the execution of Clarence Dunsmore's will.

"And is it your opinion, Doctor," Grimes pressed, "that a man such as Mr. Dunsmore, suffering from a concussion as a result of the fall from his horse—"

"Objection, Your Honor! The witness hasn't stated that Mr. Dunsmore was suffering from a concussion. That seems to be the diagnosis of Mr. Grimes, who is hardly a doctor."

Hatch waved an impatient hand. "Get on with it, Grimes."

The lawyer obeyed, and Kirby continued to fulfill his given function. Yes, it was likely, indeed virtually a certainty, that Mr. Dunsmore had suffered a concussion from his fall. And, having sustained such an injury, he would naturally not be able to understand the extent of his property and holdings, nor to know the natural objects of his bounty, nor to make competent decisions concerning disposition of his assets. He would be quite unable to put his affairs in order.

"That's all, Your Honor," Grimes concluded.

"Well, ma'am, ask your questions," Hatch directed.

From that last spiel of answers Prudence knew that the good doctor was no stranger to testifying in court. She studied him as she rose to her feet.

"Doctor," she began, "isn't it true there are different levels of severity to concussions?"

"That's correct, although I would hardly expect a layman to understand the medical details."

"Just answer the questions. Isn't it also true that not all blows to the head result in concussions?"

"A relatively light blow wouldn't cause a concussion."

"Is it possible that Mr. Dunsmore didn't suffer a concussion at all?"

"Quite unlikely, in my opinion."

"But possible. Just as it's also possible for a person suffering from a mild concussion to continue to conduct his affairs?"

"Not to the extent of being able to write his own will."

"That's just your opinion."

"My professional opinion."

He was slick, Prudence conceded to herself. "Are you being paid to testify here today?" she asked then.

"Why, yes, just as I expect to be paid any time I give a medical opinion or treat a patient."

"Did you ever treat Clarence Dunsmore?"

"No, ma'am."

"Was he ever a patient of yours?"

"No."

"Doctor, I may not be able to understand medical details, but even a layman like me knows that it helps to examine someone before you diagnose him!"

Her sally garnered a round of chuckles from the spectators. But Hatch, she noticed, maintained his usual courtroom glower.

She kept after the doctor a while longer, but she figured she'd already made any points she was going to score. "No further questions," she said at last.

"You got anything else, Grimes?" Hatch demanded.

He popped up like a child's wind-up toy. "No, Your Honor." He preened as he resumed his seat.

Hatch glared wordlessly at Prudence.

"I would like to call a witness now," she answered his unspoken query.

"Hop to it!"

"I call Blake Dunsmore to the stand."

She had the satisfaction of seeing Grimes lose a bit of his composure, as if he hadn't really taken her at her word the day before. But he made no objection as the Sooner Kid strutted up to take the stand. A smirk rode his ragged features.

Thaddeus went through the formalities of swearing him in as a witness. Prudence found her eyes drawn to Stark. She was always intensely aware of his presence—sometimes to the point of distraction—when he watched her in the courtroom. But at the moment he had his gaze fixed on the witness.

There was no more expression in his gray eyes and hard face than would've been there had he been staring at a fence post. However, that very lack of emotion brought a chill to Prudence's heart. Then Jim, perhaps sensing her attention, glanced her way and let his mouth quirk in a brief tight grin of encouragement.

She faced the Kid with her spirit renewed.

"When was the last time you saw your father?"

"Well, I'm not sure I recollect exactly, but it would've been a few weeks before his death."

"A few weeks?" Prudence echoed. "Don't you mean a few years? Or several years?"

"Nope, it was a couple of weeks ago, I'd say."

"And what was the occasion?"

"You see, honey—"

"Keep a civil tongue in your mouth, 'boy!" Hatch snapped.

The Kid suppressed a snarl and started over. "My pa and me had a regular routine set up where we'd meet on the trail. We had to do that way on account of my stepmom. She didn't approve of my pa seeing his own son."

The man's gall was enormous, Prudence mused. "Do you have witnesses to any of these meetings?"

"Sure, lots of them. My men, for example."

"Your men?" Prudence was quick to see what might be an opening. "What men are those?"

The Kid shifted in his chair. Of a sudden he had the look of a calf that sees the loop coming, but doesn't know how to evade it.

"Your Honor, this is irrelevant!" Grimes could also see down the trail his client had inadvertently stumbled onto.

"Shut up, Grimes," Hatch gave him short shrift. "Answer the lady's question, Mister."

The Kid's ragged features seemed to curl a little tighter as he scowled. "I've got some men who ride with me. They're back in the hills."

"Are you their leader?"

As she had guessed, his pride wouldn't let him deny it. He squared his shoulders. "Yep. They follow me, do what I tell them."

"How large is your gang?"

"Objection!" Grimes chimed in on cue. "He said nothing about a gang—just employees."

"How many gang employees do you have?" Prudence amended promptly."

"She is mischaracterizing my client's words!"

"I can see what she's doing," Hatch rumbled ominously. "Leave her to it."

"How many, Mr. Dunsmore?" Prudence persisted.

"Depends. Around a dozen or so most of the time, I'd say."

"And how do you make your living as the Sooner Kid?"

"Relevancy, Your Honor!" Grimes protested.

"It goes to his possible motivation for seeking to overturn the will!" Prudence was quick to counter.

"You heard the question," Hatch spoke to the Kid.

"We do jobs, herding cattle and such."

"Whose cattle?"

"Whoever hires us!" The Kid was clearly not happy with being questioned in this fashion by an uppity lady lawyer.

He was about to get more unhappy, Prudence thought with satisfaction. "Isn't it true that your livelihood consists, in fact, of engaging in various criminal acts and illegal enterprises?"

"That's a lie!"

"And aren't you wanted in the State of Kansas on various criminal counts? And isn't this a Wanted poster issued for your arrest by that state?" She produced the document with a flourish, relishing the moment.

"That's a fake! I was framed!"

"Your Honor, this has nothing to do with the matter at hand!" Grimes tried to regain control.

While his words were still ringing, Prudence looked at the Kid. She felt the rush of satisfaction drain from her. Suddenly silent, the outlaw chieftain was glaring at her through eyes seething with a froth of anger and lust. She almost recoiled physically from the intensity of it. Her own eyes flicked automatically to Stark, and she saw him tense where he sat.

The crashing impact of the butt of Judge Hatch's pistol-grip shotgun on the bar jerked all attention to him. "Let's see that poster!" he commanded.

Wordlessly, Prudence approached and passed the wanted

circular up to him. Uninvited, Grimes joined her. His smooth face was flushed.

Hatch gripped the circular at top and bottom and peered at it as though trying to win a staredown. Then he slapped it flat on the bar so that the image of the Kid glowered sightlessly upwards.

"I've heard enough," Hatch announced.

"Your Honor!" Prudence and Grimes protested simultaneously.

Hatch rapped sharply on the bar with the shotgun butt once again. "Listen up!" he silenced any further protests. His shaggy head swung toward the Kid. "I don't like you and I don't like your sorry breed. If I had the authority I'd throw you in the hoosegow and send for Kansas to come haul your tail back up there. But that circular don't carry any weight here." He gave a disgusted shake of his head. "I'd disinherit you too if you were my pup."

He paused to draw breath. "Howsomever," he resumed, "what your sawbones said makes some sense, Grimes. A man banged up by getting thrown from his horse just might not be able to think clear enough to write up his will. Every man has a legacy of some sort he leaves behind him, and I reckon every man ought to have the right to choose who he wants to get that legacy. Miss McKay, I'm just not sure your client had the capacity to know fully what he was doing when he wrote his will.

"Now, here's my ruling. I need to see some of them folks who witnessed that will. Bring them in here, Counselor. I'll give you thirty days to produce at least one of those witnesses so I can hear what he has to say. Understand?"

From the corner of her eye Prudence caught movement among the spectators. One of the Kid's cronies—the obnoxious Tucker—rose to his feet and strode from the room. Stark's head turned sharply to follow his progress.

"I understand, Your Honor," Prudence answered Hatch. Secretly she was relieved the decision hadn't shut the doors of the courthouse in her face. "I'd ask leave to petition for further time if circumstances dictate. The witnesses were not regular associates of the decedent. We may have some trouble locating them."

"Thirty days," Hatch repeated emphatically. "That should be plenty of time. You've got the best manhunter in both territories on your payroll." He nodded in Stark's direction. "Put him to work."

Prudence was wise enough not to press the issue.

"And I expect your client to behave in the meantime, Grimes," Hatch addressed her opponent. "If these ladies and their gentleman friend stay here in town while their man is running down the witnesses, then they're under my personal protection. Savvy?"

"Yes, sir. But I assure you my client is a peaceable and law-abiding citizen, despite the scurrilous accusations leveled against him by opposing counsel."

"Save that spiel for another trial, Counselor. Just see that he abides by the law here, or I'll land on him with both feet. Thaddeus and me will be keeping an eye on him. You hear that, Thaddeus?"

"Yes, Judge," the bailiff answered from his table.

"Court's shut down." Hatch banged the bar, using his fist this time. The structure shook.

Stark reached Prudence's side as she returned to her table. "I can ride out today," he said tersely. "That roadhouse will be a good place to start."

"I'll be ready," Prudence said.

Turning away from her, Stark wheeled back. "What?"

"I'm going with you," Prudence declared flatly, and braced herself.

It didn't matter. Stark caught her elbow and hustled her into a private card room off the main chamber. It was the most physical contact she'd had with him in recent memory—since the night they had gone dancing and ended up not speaking to one another for a week. She couldn't even remember the reason for that quarrel.

She knew the reason for this one, however, and she was determined not to back down.

"You're talking loco!" Stark exclaimed. "That roadhouse is a den of thieves and worse. Corralling those witnesses could be dangerous!"

"I'm not worried; I'll be with you," she said simply. And her words were true enough, she reflected.

The backhanded compliment bounced off of his broad chest. "I don't want you riding into danger!"

"I've ridden into danger before. And you need me on this trip. I can assess the witnesses' value to the case. I can take affidavits, if need be. I know," she hurried to override his objection, "you've had experience doing the same thing for the Pinkertons. But I've had more experience, and it's my profession."

Stark fumed wordlessly for a moment. "Why are you

always so blamed determined to look for trouble?" he demanded then.

"Well, that's certainly the pot calling the kettle black!" she snapped.

"Difference is, trouble's my profession."

"And this is my case!" she said sharply, then softened her tones. "Please, Jim. It's the best way I can serve my clients. I couldn't wait here or in Guthrie while you're out beating the bushes for witnesses that I should've had the foresight to bring here in the first place."

He glowered, but she could tell he was weakening. They'd had this same argument—or variations of it—before. She generally got her way, up to a point.

"I know the rules," she hurried on with soft insistence. "You are in charge if there's any trouble. I won't disobey your orders." She had the grace not to add that she'd sometimes even managed to be of assistance when their lives had been at risk. She knew it would occur to him without any prompting.

She saw his jaws work, and heard his teeth grind together. Instinctively, without planning it, she reached toward him. But this time, without her consicous volition, the gesture was more than the fleeting touch she usually employed. She pressed her open hand against his chest. Beneath her palm she felt the surging beat of his heart.

One of Stark's arms lifted with startling swiftness, as though to sweep her into an embrace. Her own heart surged. Emotions and desires vibrated almost palpably between them.

Stark's arm froze. Slowly his open fingers folded into a

tight fist. Still slowly, like he was struggling with effort, he lowered his arm back to his side.

Prudence withdrew her hand. It was trembling, she noted vaguely.

"You still figure this is a good idea?" Stark asked hoarsely. "With us riding together we'll be sleeping over on the trail."

Prudence knew her face flushed red. "I trust you," she said softly. *But do you trust yourself, girl?* a voice whispered in her mind with sly perception. The notion of being alone with him on the trail had unnerving appeal. "We could get someone to accompany us," she suggested aloud.

Stark sneered. "There's no time for that! And I don't need some chaperone riding herd on me."

His tone bit stingingly. "I've nothing to fear then, do I?" Prudence asked archly.

"Whatever you say! You're the boss!" He wheeled toward the door. "But don't get in my way!"

Prudence didn't feel as though she'd won anything. And, she mused a trifle ruefully, she'd certainly managed to put a damper on anything more significant than their perpetual squabbling that might've developed between them on this journey.

Just what did she want to develop? The sly voice wasn't finished yet. But, she told herself firmly, this was just part of her job. She gave her head a mental shake. Honestly, when it came to Jim Stark, sometimes she didn't know her own mind!

He jerked the door open, but stepped aside so she could

pass through first. She brushed past him, conscious of his overwhelming masculinity.

Once they were back in the courtroom, the Dunsmore women approached them. "Where do we go from here, Miss McKay?" Sarah asked apprehensively. "Do you think there's any chance of finding those witnesses in time?"

"We're going to make a good try at it," Prudence reassured her. "Mr. Stark and I will be leaving as soon as possible for Rowland's Roadhouse."

"So you're going along, too?" Donna ventured.

Prudence winced as she saw Stark's scowl deepen. She hurried on. "Yes, I feel it will speed matters along if I'm there to question the witnesses in person."

"I suppose you're right," Sarah said understandingly. "We'll certainly be praying for your success. In the meantime, what do you think we should do? Thirty days is a long time to be away from the ranch, and we'd like to return home if you think it's wise."

Before Prudence could respond, Stark spoke up tersely. "Mrs. Dunsmore, it's simply not safe for you to travel back to your ranch without protection, and I don't have time to escort you there. I can't order you to stay here in Earlsboro, but I highly recommend it—for your own protection."

"But William will be with us," Donna said, a note of pride in her voice.

"He's only one man against however many hired guns your stepbrother might choose to send against you," Prudence spoke up quickly to save Stark from making that obvious point. It was clear he wasn't in the mood for debating any more females.

"That's right," Stark agreed, his tone now a little more civil. "Besides, it's better to keep the Kid's attention focused here in Earlsboro. He'll be less likely to make a move against you here in front of so many witnesses. But if you head out on the trail home, you'll be easy targets for ambushing by any yahoo with a rifle."

Sarah's worried frown deepened. "I see your point, Mr. Stark. I guess we really don't have any choice then, do we? I suppose I'll just have to send a telegram to our foreman and ask him to look after things as best he can until we return. I hope Blake doesn't launch an attack on the ranch in the meantime to get back at Donna and me."

"I don't think he will," Prudence said reassuringly. "I'm sure at this point that pompous attorney, Grimes, has told him he stands a good chance of owning at least a portion of his father's property. So it wouldn't make any sense for him to destroy his own assets."

Stark nodded his agreement. "The only thing that would benefit him would be to reduce the number of potential heirs. So just sit tight here in town and don't take any foolish chances. Be on guard at all times for danger."

"Don't worry, Mr. Stark." Thaddeus Jenkins had approached. "The judge and I will see to their safety."

As Jim would see to hers, Prudence was sure. But as to what else might await them, or their relationship, on their mission, she hadn't the foggiest notion.

Chapter Six

Rowland's Roadhouse was pretty typical, Stark mused as he and Prudence reined their horses in at the hitching rail. Consisting of a sizeable frame building, barn and attached corral, and some scattered sheds, it was a mix of saloon, hotel, café, and general store. Rarely frequented by lawmen, such places were havens for longriders and range riffraff looking for a drink, a meal, and a temporary roof over their heads.

Stark stepped out of the saddle and gave Prudence a hand down from her mount. She hardly needed his assistance; she was no stranger to traveling horseback. In divided riding skirt, frilled blouse, and dainty Stetson, she made a comely picture. But the small revolver belted about her slender waist dispelled any notion of a helpless female. She was no stranger to handling a firearm either.

Stark paused before mounting the porch, and turned his head to speak over his shoulder to her.

"I'll stay clear if there's trouble," she anticipated him.

Stark grimaced. "Watch my back," he growled.

"That too."

It occurred to Stark that he was becoming entirely too accustomed to having her nearby when things might be rough. But he knew from experience that having her there could be worthwhile.

Her presence no longer kept him on edge fretting about her safety. Rather, it stretched his nerves to a wire-taut awareness that heightened his senses and reactions. Instinctively, he knew he was at his most dangerous when defending her. He didn't allow himself to spend much time dwelling on the deeper significance of that fact.

His boots clattered on the weathered boards of the porch as he crossed it. Left-handed, he reached for the doorknob, leaving his right hand free. Both his .45 and his bowie knife rode his belt. The .38 hideaway was tucked securely at the small of his back, concealed beneath his gunbelt.

Inside, the building was dim and dusty. To their left a pair of batwing doors led into the saloon where he saw a couple of hombres lounging at the bar. The rest of the front area was a general store. It looked to carry a little bit of everything, but specialized in weapons, tack, nonperishable food items such as jerked meat, and other gear a man might need on the trail. Especially if he was on the run. . . .

A burly bearded fellow was behind the counter, which boasted a display case with cracked glass. The glass was too grimy to make out much of what was on display.

Beneath ridges of old scar tissue left over from prizefight rings of days past, the proprietor's eyes widened a mite as he got a good look at his prospective customers. Prudence, Stark reflected, stood out like a rose in a weed patch.

"Howdy, folks." The fellow was affable enough. "What can I do for you?"

"I'm Jim Stark. This is Miss McKay. She's an attorney," Stark made the introductions. "We're looking for three fellows who served as witnesses when a man wrote his will in here a spell back. You might remember it."

"Yep, I do, for a fact. Ain't too often we get folks coming in here to write out a will."

"The witnesses were Vic Jamison, Bass Barnett, and Dade Sorley. You got any ideas as to their whereabouts these days?"

"Well, Vic Jamison is either strumming a harp or feeling some heat about now—the latter, I suspect. He was shot down in a little gun fracas right in yonder about two weeks ago." Rowland nodded toward the saloon doors.

It was a pretty poor start for their search. "What about the others?" Stark asked aloud.

"All three of them was regulars around here when they was passing through. Bass Barnett is a wrestler. Tags along with carnivals and circuses, challenging all comers to pin him in the ring, or even last three minutes. Does some strong-man stunts too. I seen him pick up a blacksmith and slam him down like he was a sack of feed in here one night when they'd had a difference of opinion. Barnett's a rough one. That blacksmith didn't get up for a spell."

"Where is he now?"

"Not sure. Last I heard he was with a carney down around Lenora."

The Pearl of the Prairies, as the residents were prone to call it, maybe as a joke. It was anything but that, Stark mused. But it was a rough-and-ready town where a bruiser like Barnett wouldn't have any trouble drawing a crowd to watch him perform. To get there, he and Prudence were looking at a long haul.

"What about Dade Sorley?"

"Hard to say. He's a drifter, does odd jobs, like riding as a security guard, when he's not dealing cards or making fool wagers. Haven't seen him here since that night, come to think of it."

Stark chewed it over. They didn't have much to go on.

"Can you give us any idea at all?" Prudence spoke up.

Whether it was feminine appeal or interrogation skill, Stark didn't care to guess, but Rowland gave the matter serious thought, scowling so the scar tissue drew down to almost cover his eyes.

"Hang on," he said at last and left the counter to cross to the batwing doors. "Any of you fellows know where Dade Sorley's keeping himself these days? Lady attorney in here is looking for him."

Stark heard a muffled chorus of denials. Shrugging, Rowland returned to the counter. "Check the trouble towns, is about the best I can tell you," he advised Prudence.

That didn't narrow things down a whole lot, Stark thought sourly. "Tell me more about Vic Jamison," he requested aloud. "Who killed him, and why?" He felt Prudence's speculative gaze touch him.

"Fellow name of Luke Taylor. There'd been bad blood between them for years. Finally came to a head. Everybody around here knew one of them was bound to end up dead if they ever tangled."

Thankfully his half-formed hunch had proven false, Stark concluded. There was no connection between Jamison's death and his witnessing of the will. That being the case, there wasn't much left for him and Prudence here.

Except some trouble, he amended the thought as he saw one of the saloon's patrons swaggering in their direction. Behind him a handful of cronies looked on eagerly. Stark cut a glance at Rowland. Affable and helpful the proprietor might be, but he wasn't going to cross one of his regulars. He was backing away, keeping his face expressionless. He refused to meet Stark's eye.

"The man says you're a lady lawyer," the hardcase addressed Prudence without preliminary. "How'd you like to handle my case?" He chuckled crudely.

Prudence gazed coolly up at him. "Who did you murder?"

The fellow grinned. "Murder ain't what I got on my mind, honey."

"I'm sorry." Prudence stepped deftly aside so her suitor found himself facing Stark. "I already have a client."

Undaunted, the hardcase pressed forward until he and Stark were chest to chest. He was as tall as Stark, and as broad. Blood-shot eyes grew narrow in his whiskered face.

"You looking for trouble, pilgrim?" he growled.

Stark lifted his open hands and stepped back. "No trouble, friend," he said.

The hardcase sneered and opened his mouth to speak.

Stark shut it with his boot. He'd stepped back to gain room, and his leg flew up, hinging on his knee in the high front kick of *savate*. The heel of his boot drove the yahoo's jaw shut, snapped his head back, and lifted him off his feet to fling him sprawling senseless on the board floor. Distracted by Stark's uplifted hands, he'd never seen it coming.

Stark shot a look at Rowland. The burly proprietor had gone pale. "You're *that* Jim Stark," he muttered in sudden understanding.

Stark swung his gaze toward the saloon doors. The hardcase's pack members had beat a hasty retreat back into their den, leaving the batwing doors swinging behind them. Stark let himself relax a notch. Prudence's face was a pale lovely mask.

"I'm sorry, Mr. Stark," Rowland began lamely. "If I'd known it was you—"

"You'd have been frightened into behaving like a man," Stark finished for him coldly. "Obliged for the information." He resisted the urge to put his foot through the dusty glass of the store counter. "Let's shake the dust off our heels," he addressed Prudence.

"Was that absolutely necessary?" she queried tightly once they were outside. "It was a bit extreme."

"Could be I saved his life by kicking his teeth in," Stark returned shortly. "I might've had to shoot our way out if I hadn't nipped it in the bud." He paused a moment before adding, "None of this would've happened if you hadn't insisted upon tagging along."

She ducked her head. "You're right," she admitted softly. "Maybe this wasn't such a good idea after all."

Stark kicked himself mentally. Her contrition was totally unexpected and largely unjustified. She did have a right to be here, and the trouble had come through no fault of her own. There'd been plenty of times when he'd stirred up a ruckus all by himself. Truth be told, he enjoyed her company more than he was readily willing to confess.

"Forget it," he growled. "We better make tracks for Lenora."

The next morning they began the first stage of their journey by rail, with the horses riding in the stock car. As he sat beside Prudence in the crowded passenger car, Stark tried to relax and enjoy the change of transportation. The plush velvet cushions were certainly a welcome departure from the hard saddle leather they'd been pounding the past few days.

He sighed. They'd done a lot of hard riding for very little results. He hoped their luck would change at Lenora.

Beside him, Prudence sat pensively staring out the window at the prairie lands flowing past. They'd spent the night in a passably nice hotel before boarding the train, and she appeared well-rested. A good thing, too. The toughest part of their quest likely lay ahead of them.

He still regretted his outburst of temper the night before at the roadhouse. He needed to apologize, but he had no idea how to lead into it.

All of a sudden she turned toward him and caught him

watching her. He smiled in spite of himself when their eyes met. She smiled in return.

"Bet I know what you were thinking just now," she said teasingly. "How much easier this trek would be without having to drag me along, right?"

He was more than a little relieved to see she'd regained her plucky attitude. The hardest thing he'd had to deal with was that his thoughtless outburst had hurt her feelings. But apparently she wasn't as crushed as he'd feared.

He tried to match her lighthearted tone. "Naw, I wasn't thinking that at all. I was just sitting here enjoying the scenery, like you were. Only the thought crossed my mind that one of the prettiest sights was right here *inside* the car."

Predictably, a blush stained her cheeks, but she didn't look away. "All right, what are you up to?" She tried to sound stern. "Compliments like that usually come out of an ulterior motive."

He shrugged. "Nope. The compliment's genuine. I'm simply trying to make amends for my short temper at the roadhouse. I shouldn't have blamed you for what happened. I like having you along. It's nice having such pleasant company to travel with.

Her eyes searched his. "Oh, Jim, do you mean that?"

She looked so pleased with his words that he reached for her hand and gave it a squeeze. "Yes, Miss McKay, I mean that sincerely."

"Thank you." Her blush deepened considerably, and she looked quickly out the window again. "Oklahoma has a beauty all its own, doesn't it?" she said breathlessly. "It's not at all spectacular like some of the surrounding states, but it has a sort of quiet, robust dignity. The sameness of the prairie is comforting somehow. Like spending time with a good friend."

Stark had no idea why her comments seemed appropriate to the moment or why they pricked his heart as they did. He just leaned his head back against the plush velvet seat and gave her hand another squeeze.

The woman sure knew how to accept an apology graciously.

The town of Lenora had been established shortly after the opening of the Cheyenne-Arapaho Lands for settlers. It was a bustling community of several hundred citizens, which easily made it the largest population center in the area.

At rail's end Stark and Prudence switched to horseback and reached the town late the next afternoon. Prudence was flagging a little, but she shook off Stark's suggestion of getting a meal and finding accomodations for the night.

"Let's try to locate Barnett first," she insisted. "Listen, I think I can hear caliope music. It must be coming from the carnival. Thank heavens we got here before it moved on. Come on." She kicked her mare into motion and headed in the direction of the music. Stark followed along.

They cut through the central section of town, joining with a growing exodus of folks drifting in the direction of the music. Businesses crowded Main Street: the Hotel Daisy, the North Star Saloon, the Rickart Brothers Saddlery, the Lenora State Bank, and a collection of stores.

But the town had a rough reputation. Stark recalled the aging town lawman of local legend who'd hung up his guns when, on his eighty-sixth birthday, he'd failed to drill a dime pitched into the air as a target.

Booths and tents housing the sideshows and games had been set up around the big top where the show would be held later in the evening. The carney was already doing a good business. The yelling of kids and the haranguing of barkers mingled with the music. A fine haze of dust hung in the air. The varied scents of fried foods made Stark's belly remind him it had been a spell since it had been filled.

"There," Stark said as he spotted the elevated wrestling ring surrounded by a mostly male crowd. A match was already under way. Two bare-chested figures grappled in the center of the ring.

Dismounting at a handy hitching rail, Stark shouldered his way through the press with Prudence close in his wake. He halted at the edge of the platform where he had a clear view of the occupants.

"This seems familiar," Prudence murmured unhappily at his shoulder.

It wasn't hard to tell the two combatants apart. Bass Barnett—Bruiser Barnett, according to a frayed banner strung above the ring—was a giant, bullet-headed man with sleek sculpted muscles that flexed and rolled and bunched at times into ugly knots as he shifted and countered. His pate was shaved bald—likely to prevent any opponent from grabbing his hair. His massive legs were clad in striking red tights. Sweat gleamed on his bare torso.

His opponent—or victim—was almost as big. He carried the heavy functional slabs of muscle that came from long hours of lifting and toting. No doubt he was the champion in contests between local farm boys.

But he wasn't in the ring with another farm boy. He'd paid his money to go up against a professional. Bruises and scrapes on his arms and shoulders showed he'd hit the canvas more than once.

They'd come together in a test of raw strength. Their hands were clasped overhead, fingers interlaced. Their muscles strained as each strove to bend the other over backward. And Barnett was stretching it out, Stark understood as he watched. The carney wrestler was putting on a show for the locals.

There was a trick that could be used by a grappler from that position. By bending an opponent's hands sharply back on his wrists, a weaker man could force a stronger man to yield through pain alone rather than brute strength.

Barnett didn't need the trick. Stark could tell by the slight tremor that raced over his perspiring body when he truly began to exert his full power. Slowly, as inexorable as the death of the buffalo, the local champion was bent backward. Farther and farther he was pushed until his spine formed a straining arch that human bone and tissue were never meant to sustain.

At last, with a strangled cry of pain and frustration, the fellow crumpled sidewise, going almost to one knee. Immediately Barnett released him and moved back with a step that was almost dainty.

Face suffused with rage, the farm boy kept his feet and drew erect. Barnett tossed his head to invite him back in.

The fellow took the invite. He lunged, guarding with his

left, as he swept a long right arm out and around to clamp his fingers on the nape of Barnett's bull neck.

This time Barnett didn't stoop to matching strength with him. Before the fingers could secure a grip, he twisted his body deftly. His left hand came up swiftly under his foe's extended right arm and spun him halfway about as Barnett ducked clear. For maybe a heartbeat the challenger's back was unprotected.

Barnett pounced. Like twin boa constrictors, his arms slipped under the yokel's armpits, then lifted so his hands could link behind the fellow's neck. A full nelson.

"Give it up, boy," Barnett grunted. "Ain't no way this hold can be broken!"

If the hold could be broken, the plowboy wasn't the one to do it. He flailed helplessly as Barnett, plainly getting a kick out of his supremacy, forced the other man's straining neck to bend relentlessly until his chin was pressed against his chest. And still Barnett bore down.

Stark felt a grim chill. Beside him, Prudence had caught her breath. An ugly rumble was beginning to rise from the ranks of the spectators. Much more, and the farm boy's neck would be snapped clean.

Abruptly Barnett relented. He jerked his hands back and snaked his arms from under those of his foe. The hapless plowboy collapsed like a crumpled gunny sack.

"The winner, and still undefeated!" A scrawny oldster in a threadbare suit appeared of a sudden. Clearly he was Barnett's barker and token referee. "Let's give the champion a rest," he admonished the crowd. "Spread the word; every half hour, Bruiser Barnett takes on all comers!"

The crowd began to drift toward other sideshows. Stark doubted Barnett would get too many more challengers after the brutal work he'd done on the local favorite. He noticed the barker scowling at the wrestler behind his back. The plowboy was being helped out of the ring by a couple of his pals.

Still in the ring, Barnett shrugged into a flannel shirt against the coolness brought on by the gathering dusk. After a moment he noticed Stark and Prudence waiting outside the ring.

"Got a minute?" Stark queried.

Barnett eyed Prudence. "I reckon."

If nothing else, Stark reflected dryly, having Prudence along sure seemed to make folks more willing to palaver. Male folks, anyway.

Barnett clambered agilely from the ring, and dropped lightly to the ground from the platform. Up close he bulked taller and wider than Stark. "What can I do for you?" His voice was a rumble from a cave.

Stark did the talking. He saw Barnett's eyes narrow briefly as he introduced himself. The wrestler stopped paying so much attention to Prudence.

"That's the whole of it," Stark finished. "We need you back at Earlsboro in three weeks' time. We've got a subpoena if need be, but we'll make it worth your while if you come on your own."

Barnett was eyeing Stark, sizing him up like they were in the ring. "I got a deal," he proposed at last.

"Let's hear it."

There was a cunning light in Barnett's eyes that puzzled Stark. "I'll go be your witness on one condition."

"I'm listening."

"You and me in the ring. Win, lose, or draw, and I'll go with you. Otherwise, no deal. Your clients can lose everything, far as I'm concerned, subpoena or no subpoena."

Stark heard Prudence's sharply indrawn breath. "Done," he said before she could speak.

"Here and now," Barnett demanded.

Stark shrugged. "The sooner the better. What rules?"

Barnett grinned wickedly. "Best man wins."

"Suits me," Stark said.

Chapter Seven

The barker was summoning the crowd back, making a lot of noise about the upcoming match between Bruiser Barnett and the Peacemaker. Folks were starting to gather.

"Way I see it," Barnett was explaining, the cunning gleam still in his eyes, "if I can whip you then it's a great big feather in my cap. You're top dog in these parts nowadays. Everyone knows about how you took that no-holds-barred prizefight ring apart, beat their top man from back East. If I can whip you, it'll be my ticket out of these sideshow matches and into the big time!"

Barnett's plan had a fairly sound basis, Stark allowed. He knew wrestling was almost as popular as prizefighting in some parts of America and in Europe. "Good luck," he said dryly.

Barnett chuckled coarsely. "My good luck will be your

bad luck, bounty hunter!" With no more ado, he shrugged out of his shirt and climbed back in the ring.

The barker was taking bets. Stark couldn't tell how the odds were running. There was at least some sentiment for seeing the carney wrestler taught a lesson. He hoped he was the man to do it.

He started to unbutton his shirt. Turning, he met Prudence's skeptical gaze.

"None of this makes any sense! Why does he want to fight you?" she demanded.

Stark shrugged. "You heard him. It's about beefing up his reputation. He thinks he'll be a bigger draw if he whips me. And you'll have to admit he's right. You can't fault him for wanting to move up from this two-bit operation."

"No, but I can fault you for going along with his plan! Why put yourself in danger like this and risk serious injury? You saw what he did to that other poor man, who, by the way, was much bigger than you are!"

"Sometimes brawn doesn't count for as much as brains."

"So we finally get to your real motive. You're just itching to tangle with him, aren't you? You probably have some misguided idea about evening the score for all the farmhands and blacksmiths Barnett has victimized in the ring, right?"

"Look, do you want him for a witness or not?" Stark's retort was sharp. "Those are his terms. A subpoena doesn't meant a cotton-picking thing to him. It's this, or taking him back by force."

"There's not much difference that I can see!"

Stark scowled silently down at her and shucked his shirt. The evening air was cool on his bare chest. She was partly right, he admitted to himself. And if he could give Barnett a taste of his own medicine in the process, all the better. He felt a ripple of anticipation at matching strength and cunning with the bigger man.

Prudence gave a resigned sigh. "Oh, good grief! Let me have your shirt." She extended a hand for the garment. Their fingertips brushed as she took it. His fingers were left tingling.

Then, out of the blue, she moved a small step closer and stood on tiptoe. He felt her softness against him, the light touch of her hand on his chest, and the quick press of her lips on his cheek.

Just as quickly, she drew back. Her expression was about as startled as his own, Stark reckoned.

"Please don't let him hurt you," she managed in a soft breathless tone.

"You don't need to worry. I'll be fine," Stark said automatically, giving her arm a reassuring squeeze.

"I'll still worry. Give me your belt—your gunbelt." Like the shift of a contrary prairie breeze, she was back to sounding irritated with him.

Wordlessly he complied with her order, adding the .38 to the load of weaponry she now toted. He pulled off his boots slowly and dropped them at her feet. For a moment longer he hesitated.

"Oh, go on and fight!" she said.

"Yeah."

Stark clambered through the ropes. He couldn't afford to be distracted by whatever had just happened, he told himself. Whipping Barnett was a tall order, especially while he fancied he could still feel the touch of Prudence's lips on his cheek.

And Barnett sure didn't look like he was interested in playing it out to please the rubes this time. Hunched, he lunged, seeking a hold, any hold, because if they ever came to grips, Stark would be outclassed.

Barnett almost got his hold. Stark stood rooted until the last possible chance, then ripped an uppercut between Barnett's reaching arms. The wrestler's bullet head rocked back on his thick neck, and Stark felt the impact of knuckles on jawbone all the way to his shoulder. Ninety out of a hundred men would've dropped from that blow, but Stark was betting Barnett was one of the other ten. He stepped back and wheeled clear.

He would've won the bet.

Barnett faltered, but caught himself in mid-lunge, and whirled fast enough so that Stark's second blow only skidded painfully off his artfully ducked head. Stark kicked him in the leg, swivelling to put force behind his foot. He had to slow this behemoth down. He tried for the knee, but landed low. Still, it gave him time to duck past Barnett and lift a right to his ear a half-heartbeat before sinking a left under his ribs. He felt only hefty muscles with no give there. The man was as solid as a boulder.

But the boulder moved with surprising speed. Barnett's grasping fingers seemed to burn Stark's flesh as he evaded yet another darting snatch of one big hand. He hooked with his foot, driving it up under the ribs where he'd just punched. A little give this time; he needed to use his feet and keep his distance from that menacing grip.

He faded away, never going straight backward, but circling, sidestepping, sliding along the ropes. And as he did he stabbed and thrust with his feet—first one, then the other, or doubling up with one. The tree-trunk legs, the solid lower body, even the reaching arms were his targets, and his feet sliced the air to smack into flesh and muscle.

But Barnett was no greenhorn at cornering a foe in the ring. He feinted sideways with his whole body, shifted, sidestepped, and suddenly Stark was backed up against the ringpost. Barnett's widespread arms blocked any escape. The wrestler bared his teeth and came in.

Stark had only an instant to brace his back against the flimsy cornerpost and pray that it held. He grabbed a ring rope with either hand, and as Barnett lunged at him, he reared back and shot both feet out. Barnett saw the tactic and tried too late to grab his legs. Stark's feet rammed full on into his chest and face.

He lurched backward. Stark dropped his feet back to the floor, and, now that Barnett was slowed up, tried for a head shot with a high circular snapping kick that pivoted his body halfway about as he threw it. His right foot booted Barnett's head ninety degrees, but he'd overestimated the damage he'd done to the wrestler.

Like the jaws of a trap, Barnett's big hands shot up to clamp about foot and ankle, imprisoning Stark's leg at full extension of the kick. Instantly, Barnett set himself and heaved, swinging Stark's entire body into the air. Stark sensed the move coming and went with it, kicking off with his anchor leg. His left foot clipped Barnett's jaw in passing as the wrestler flung him sailing across the ring.

Fire seared Stark's hip joint. He crashed down, at the last moment managing the old ring trick of slapping with his arms to break the fall. Still, the impact seemed to rattle his teeth in their sockets.

He surged up onto his feet, his vision spinning. He glimpsed Barnett already nearly upon him, and tried to wheel clear. He was too slow on his wrenched leg. Barnett's hand shot out to grasp his wrist. Despite his best efforts he was in the monster's clutches.

It was the last place he wanted to be. Barnett yanked him forward. Stark stomped on his foot, punched to his gut, banged his forehead down into Barnett's face. Barnett shook it all off. The fingers of his other hand closed like manacles on the imprisoned arm. Deftly he whipped Stark about, levering the trapped arm up behind Stark's back in a hammerlock.

Before Barnett could exert full pressure, before he could let go with one hand to catch the elbow of Stark's free left arm, Stark lifted that arm and twisted to his own left, swiveling at the waist so that he was almost face to face with his captor. He dropped his left arm over Barnett's arms, clamping them against his own body. He felt his right arm pull free with the swift turn of his body, and he used that fist to uppercut to Barnett's jaw.

The move should've freed him. But it wasn't that easy; not against Barnett. Somehow, before he could pull clear, Barnett managed to snare his other arm. Stark's strength was no match for him. In a trice, Barnett had entwined his free arm under and then over to secure an arm bar. With Stark's arm tangled in both of his, he bore down hard.

For Stark it was yield or lose that arm. It might be dislocated, broken, crippled permanently. He bent his legs, letting himself be forced over backward. As his shoulders met the canvas, he drew his knees to his chin and somersaulted backward.

The motion pulled his arm free, though it felt as if some of his skin was left behind. He rolled up onto his feet on shaky legs. Barnett was just straightening, and Stark lifted a knee to his jaw. Barnett was staggered, but Stark felt almost like a puppet supported by slackening strings. He wanted to sag to the floor.

Instead he tried to skip sidewise. His feet tangled, and Barnett had him again. He was whirled about like a scarecrow in a twister. He glimpsed the avid faces of the crowd blurring past. Then Barnett's massive arms came up under his own, and the wrestler's fingers interlaced themselves on the back of his skull. Barnett grunted in ugly triumph.

A full nelson, the unbreakable hold. Barnett had him in it.

During that first instant of the massive surge of Barnett's applying pressure, as he seemed to feel a red-hot poker jammed down his spinal column, Stark knew with a terrifying certainty that this was no longer a simple sideshow match. For whatever reason, Barnett was fixing to kill him.

Understanding pumped strength into Stark's sinews. As the brutal pressure on his spine increased, he swung his outspread arms together as if trying to clap his hands in front of his face. At the same time he smashed his head back into Barnett's face. He felt the wrestler's hold slacken by a fraction, and he bent forward at the waist, going with the terrible pressure, and sidestepping so he could get his right leg in back of Barnett's right leg. Shoving his knee behind that of Barnett, he buckled the bigger man's leg. Straightening then, he swung his right arm, stiff as a fireplace poker, across the broad bare chest behind him. His balance broken, his leverage lost, Barnett crashed over backwards as Stark surged free from his flailing arms.

No way to break it, huh? Stark thought with savage satisfaction.

He whirled and fell on Barnett's midriff with both knees. Stunned by the abrupt reversal of his fortunes, Barnett was caught unawares. The air went out of him as though he'd been punctured. The crowd was frozen.

Stark straddled him, a knee pinning each arm to the canvas. One hand shot down and gripped Barnett's throat. Stark cocked his other fist.

"Blast you!" he rasped. "You were trying to kill me! Why?"

Barnett was whipped, mentally and physically. There was no resistance left in him.

"Fellow paid me," he croaked. "Told me you might be snooping around. Gave me two hundred dollars downpayment. Promised two hundred more if I did you in."

"And you figured to do it in the ring and call it an accident," Stark growled. "Who was it? Who hired you?"

"Don't know. Never seen him before. Looked like some old buffalo hunter or wolfer."

Stark eased up. "You be at that hearing," he advised coldly. "If I have to come looking for you, this little fracas will seem like a picnic. Savvy?"

"Yeah, sure," Barnett gasped. "How'd you come out of that? Never seen anybody escape a full nelson."

"There's a lot you ain't seen. And even more you don't want to see. Remember that. Now, get up."

Grunting with pain, Barnett complied. "You hurt me," he moaned.

"Not yet I didn't. Maybe next time."

Barnett shook his head. "No next time for me."

The crowd had been silent, trying to grasp what was going on in the ring. Now, with both men back on their feet, they began to react. There weren't many tears being shed for his foe, Stark noted without much regret.

Well-wishers crowded about him as he left the ring. He had his back slapped and his hand wrung a half dozen times as he shouldered through the ranks. Apparently a good many of the spectators had made money on the match.

Prudence had withdrawn to the edge of the crowd. Her eyes were bright, but she was crisp and businesslike as she returned his belongings to him. The fleeting kiss she planted on his cheek might've been a fantasy.

"What was going on after you had him down?" she asked almost sharply as he buttoned his shirt. "You were talking to him. What were you saying?"

"The match was nothing but a scheme to let him get his hands on me," Stark told her.

Her brow furrowed in puzzlement. "What do you mean?"

Stark eyed the gathering gloom of the night. Was Barnett all by his lonesome, or had others been recruited to do the job if he failed? Easy enough to find hardcases willing to earn big money for the cost of a bullet. Or two. Prudence would be the second obvious target. The shadows, the commotion of the carnival, would make it easy for another hired killer to do his job.

"Let's clear out of this sorry town first," he evaded her query. "Then I'll tell you."

She started to protest, but studied him for a moment and nodded. "Whatever you say."

Stark kept his head turning, his eyes shifting as he looked this way and that. His palm hovered near the butt of his Colt.

Some of the uneasiness left him once they had their horses under them, and Lenora was fading into the darkened prairie on their backtrail.

"Seems the Sooner Kid must've sicced somebody on us to keep us from finding the witnesses," Stark said at last. "Like any good hunter, he set a trap. Barnett was both the bait and the trigger. What it means is we'll have to be looking over our shoulders from now on."

"And it means Dade Sorley, the remaining witness, might be in danger as well," Prudence added with quick understanding. "That's why you asked questions about Vic Jamison's death. You suspected that he might've been killed by a—a hunter hired by the Kid."

"It figured as a possiblity," Stark confirmed. "Didn't pan out that way though."

"So who is this hunter? Do you know him?"

"You might say that. Met him, leastways. His name is Talon."

Chapter Eight

Seated on a tree stump, Stark winced as he lifted his arm to scrape the keen blade of the razor down his lathered cheek.

"Good morning," Prudence called as she emerged from her tent. She must have seen him flinch. Her voice had a quick concern. "Oh, what's wrong?"

"I guess Barnett wrenched my shoulder a bit when we were tusseling," Stark answered gruffly. He was embarrassed that she had seen the sign of weakness in him.

"Here, let me help you," she said matter-of-factly. And before he quite realized what she intended, she had positioned herself behind him and plucked the straight-edge razor from his fingers. "Hold still."

She wielded the razor with a smooth efficiency. He felt the touch of her fingers as she tilted his head slightly. The heady scent of woman, mingled with the sweet smell of violets, filled his nostrils. She had not yet done up her hair for the trail, so it fell past her shoulders, brushing the back of his neck occassionally as she worked.

"Hold still, I said," she admonished.

"You didn't learn this in law school," Stark commented, moving only his lips as he spoke.

"When I was a little girl my father used to let me shave him. I'm afraid I may have left permanent scars, but he never complained. And eventually I got better." She made a final stroke of the razor. "There, all done. And not a wound in sight." She sounded quite proud of herself. "Now, which shoulder is it?"

He stiffened as her fingers probed. "That one. But it's nothing."

"Nonsense. You need some liniment on it, especially if we run into more trouble. Take your shirt off, and I'll be right back."

She was mighty good at giving orders, Stark mused sourly. Then remembering the touch of her hands, the enticing scent of her, he obeyed her command.

She rummaged in the gear and returned in a moment. Her delicate hands were surprisingly strong as she kneaded the ointment into his shoulder and neck.

"Did you do this for your father, too?"

"Sometimes."

"Well, you'll make some man a fine—Ow!"

"Sorry," Prudence said in a tone that was anything but contrite. "Go on with what you were saying."

"I was just going to say a fine . . . *attorney*."

Prudence snorted. "I thought for once you were going to compliment my finely honed domestic skills."

"I'll be happy to . . . if I ever witness them."

She gave his shoulder another sharp jab with her thumb. "Very funny. I don't know why I even try to patch you up. You'll just find some other excuse to take some foolish risk. I thought Barnett was going to break your neck."

"So did I," Stark admitted.

"You didn't have to fight him, you know."

Stark shifted under her ministrations. "Now she tells me," he muttered.

"I told you then, too," she declared emphatically. "Okay, I'm finished. Put on your shirt." Her voice sounded a bit breathless.

Stark stood up and turned around. She was only a couple of feet from him, and she didn't move away. He could take her in his arms easily, Stark thought. He sensed her thoughts were running in the same direction. Her pretty features looked almost frightened.

They were camped in a secluded draw in the prairie, miles from Lenora, miles from anywhere.

They'd ridden this narrow emotional trail before, both of them, careful to never stray far off it, fearful of the commitments and the consequences if they did.

To Stark, she was as contrary and as spirited as a range-bred filly. Whatever man corralled her would have a prize beyond value. But that man would have to pay a price in lost freedom. Because marriage to Prudence McKay would be a day-to-day, hour-to-hour battle of wits and wills—with no clear winner at the end of each skirmish.

Did he want to be that man? Was he up to such a battle? Was the prize he would gain worth the price he would pay? Something told him it was. Still . . .

"We better hit the saddles," he said hoarsely.

She let out a long breath. "Yes. I'll strike the tent." Her tone sounded at once disappointed and relieved.

He felt some disappointment himself.

But she seemed pleasant enough when they were ready to ride out. "Where do we start our search for Mr. Dade Sorley?" she asked.

"You heard what the man said. Check the trouble towns for him. Corner, Violet Springs, Keokuk Falls, Sod Town. There's plenty to choose from."

"What's the closest?"

Stark squinted thoughtfully. "That'd be Ingersoll, northeast of here."

She reined her mare about. "Let's go."

As they rode, Stark reflected that Ingersoll was a pretty likely spot to look for a fellow of Dade Sorley's breed. It was said the town had been born full-grown when the Choctaw Railroad reached that site in the Cherokee Outlet. In addition to a thriving business district, and despite several churches, it had seven saloons and two pool halls—earning it a reputation of catering to the gaming crowd. A sometime card slick like Dade Sorley would be right at home there.

But time was pressing them hard. The two-day ride to Ingersoll took them that much further away from Earlsboro and Judge Hatch's shotgun court. With a professional wrestler and attempted murderer as their only witness, however, they needed some credible source to back up his testimony. Dade Sorley was their best—and it looked like their only—bet.

They rode into town after dark on the second day, guided by the honky-tonk music and the lights of the gambling halls. Hours of riding and layers of trail dust lay heavily on them, but Stark knew there was no need asking if Prudence wanted to freshen up before tackling the job at hand. The determined set of her chin said it all.

"Lord, please let us find him here in this town," she entreated, glancing heavenward as they dismounted at the first saloon.

Providence smiled on them. They hit pay dirt in the third dive they visited, a rambling outfit that offered a fancy bar and prowling girls to complement the gaming tables. Tobacco smoke and whiskey fumes hung pungently in the air. Prudence wrinkled her nose in distaste and stared daggers at one of the floozies who drifted in their direction with an eye on Stark. The soiled dove beat a hasty retreat.

A crowd of noisy men had gathered around something going on at the back of the place. Stark led the way to the bar and spoke over the hubbub.

"Looking for a fellow name of Dade Sorley. Has he been around here?"

The barkeep nodded toward the crowd. "Mr. Sorley is over yonder," he answered with a stilted German accent. A lot of the settlers hereabouts were German immigrants, Stark remembered.

"What's the attraction?" he ventured.

"They're settling up on a knife-throwing contest. Mr. Sorley has wagered a large sum."

"Obliged." Stark thumbed a coin onto the bar.

As he turned away, his palm dropped down to brush the hilt of the sheathed bowie knife riding his belt.

The spectators were lined three deep. Drawing near, Stark heard the familiar thumping sound of a thrown knife sinking into solid wood. Exclamations and jeers went up from the crowd.

"You lost that one, Sorley. One more and then you've got to pay up," a man shouted with satisfaction.

"That's right, Sorley! Cash on the barrelhead!" another added with ugly glee.

Looked as though Sorley's odds hadn't played out, Stark mused as he parted the ranks of onlookers so he and Prudence could pass through.

Two men were facing a wall some fifteen feet distant. On the wall six playing cards had been tacked. Four of the cards bore a puncture dead center. From the fifth in the same spot protruded a knife. It was double-edged with a slim hilt and no guard. A throwing knife, Stark recognized, not intended for close-in fighting or much of anything else except hitting a target.

Its owner paced smoothly forward to retrieve it. He had the copper skin and black hair of Indian blood, although he wore denim breeches and a checked shirt. Likely he had learned his skills from some tribal warrior who was a veteran of the Indian Wars.

Dade Sorley—evidently the other man—was tall and

thin with a bony face. Just now his features were pale with obvious apprehension.

"How you going to pay us all off after he makes the next bulls-eye, Sorley?" one of the spectators yelled, cinching Stark's estimate of what was going on.

It was easy enough to figure. For whatever reason— maybe a gambler's compulsion to ride his luck to its death—Sorley had bet not only the knife artist, but a good number of the spectators, that the other man couldn't make six perfect throws.

From the confident ease with which the fellow was returning to the throwing line, Sorley had been wrong.

Stark glimpsed the turn of Prudence's head and briefly met her glance. He could tell they were both thinking the same thing. Here was another mighty sorry witness for their case.

Shrugging off his misgivings, he paid attention to the contest. The knife artist stood for a moment, knife dangling from his right fist. Then his grip tightened on the hilt and he lifted the knife up by his ear as he stepped forward with his left foot. Poised, he eyed his target. In a single smooth sequence then, his throwing arm went back as his left foot slid even further forward. He threw with a circular sweep of his arm, the knife slipping from his hand just before his arm reached full extension. The knife spun like a windmill—two full revolutions—before its point drove dead center through the card and a full inch into the hard wood behind it.

There was no argument that he'd won the bet. The watchers clapped and whistled and hollered. Dade Sorley stood stricken, like a rat dropped in the center of a circle of cats. The knife thrower turned slowly to face him, his copper features expressionless.

"Pay up, Dade!" somebody shouted, and a full half-dozen others joined the chorus.

Sorley was packing a six-gun, but he made no effort to go for it. Instead he lifted his hands palms out. "Listen, fellows," he stammered.

"We can take it out of your hide!" The crowd was getting ugly.

Again Stark met Prudence's gaze. If they didn't do something, and do it fast, their witness might not be in any shape to testify. Ever.

Stark stepped out of the ranks of spectators and casually out into the arena. On his second step, when all eyes were on him, he pulled his bowie and tossed it straight up. He didn't need to look to see when the heavy spinning blade reached its apex and started to fall. He didn't need to look when gauging its descent. He reached up in mid-step and plucked the whirling weapon out of the air, his hand closing firmly about the polished hardwood hilt.

A murmur of appreciation ran through the crowd. Gratified that he hadn't sliced a finger off in pulling the stunt, his face impassive, Stark surveyed the folks in the room. He caught a glimpse of Prudence. Her lovely face was set in strained lines.

"I'll make all of you a wager," he announced flatly. "One throw. I can do the same thing this hombre did, and I can do it faster. If I lose, I'll pay off what Sorley owes you. If I win, his debts to you are cancelled."

He let the offer sink in. They were a rough crowd who appreciated skill with a weapon and a winner-take-all dare.

"What's in it for you?" A burly hard case in the front ranks demanded.

Stark cut a glance at Sorley. The man had a stunned look on his face that hadn't yet matured into hope. "I've got business with him." Stark indicated Sorley. "I want him in one piece."

That got an ugly round of chuckles.

"Who are you, hombre?" The knife artist spoke for the first time. He had an accent from south of the border, so maybe some of the old Spanish hidalgos with their mastery of weapons ran in his veins as well.

"Just a man with a knife," Stark answered him. He twirled the bowie deftly.

"Three to one he can't do it!" someone in the crowd yelled.

Those might be pretty good odds, Stark mused. He'd seen how well his opponent could throw, but he hadn't seen how fast.

Still, the bet was quickly taken by another spectator. "You're on! Ten dollars to your thirty!"

That did it. The notion of the bold challenge had caught on. Bets flew fast, offers were made and accepted. His skills sure seemed to be the focus of a lot of wagering of late, Stark reflected wryly.

He put his eyes on his opponent. "Any objection?"

Wordlessly the hombre shook his head.

"What about you?" Stark addressed Sorley.

Another negative shake of a head, this one emphatic.

"I'm obliged, Mister, and I ain't asking questions. I sure hope you're as good as you say!"

"So do I."

"Luck to you."

"Thanks." Stark dismissed him and looked for Prudence again. He couldn't read any expression beyond the strain still visible on her face. She didn't approve of gambling, and he wasn't one for making bets himself, particularly of this sort. When he gambled, it was generally with his life.

Arrangements were quickly made. New cards replaced two of the punctured ones so the accuracy of the contest could be rightly judged. Some wag had selected an ace and an eight. Aces and eights: Dead Man's Hand. Hickock had been holding it when he'd gambled that no one had the nerve to try backshooting him. He'd lost.

Stark saw his opponent eyeing the bowie knife. There were those who should've known better, who said that a bowie knife wasn't worth beans for throwing. Stark gauged the distance from the target to the throwing line. It was about right, he calculated.

"Gentlemen, you will take your places." The barkeep had been summoned as caller and judge. "I will count to three and you will both throw. Is that understood?"

The knife artist stood as he had before, left foot a short step in front, throwing knife held point down, his arm hanging loose-limbed at his side. Stark stood the same way. The trick for throwing the heavy bowie—for any knife—was to know how far it took for the knife to perform a full revolution in flight. Since it was bigger and heavier than most knives, the bowie took more space. Once you had the distance down, you stood far enough from the target so the blade would reach it point first.

"One . . . two . . . three!"

From the corner of his vision, Stark saw his opponent's arm flash up and back past his ear. And he was fast.

As his foe's arm moved, Stark flipped his own knife underhand, a quick flick of his arm that launched the heavy bowie well before his opponent could complete the downward sweep of his own arm to release his knife.

Ten inch blade flashing, the bowie turned through a complete revolution and sank its point in the exact center of the ace card and over an inch into the wood behind. A heartbeat later, the throwing knife thudded into the center of the eight.

"Winner!" the barkeep's finger stabbed at Stark.

As the spectators reacted, Stark strode to the wall. Retrieving the bowie, he strolled back toward the throwing line.

His opponent eyed him as he approached. His dark, high-cheeked face was a mask. "You tricked me," he spoke through tight lips.

"No trick," Stark said. And pivoting in a single whiplash of movement, he flung the bowie overhand. Again it made its flashing turn and plunged precisely into the hole it had left in the card, driving even more deeply into the wood.

"He would've beat him either way!" one spectator shouted in awe.

Stark sauntered once more to the wall and plucked the bowie free. As he turned back, he saw the knife artist had produced another throwing blade from somewhere on his person. His eyes were black with rage and wounded pride.

"Perhaps," he spat, "you would like to try again. This time we will use each other as targets."

The crowd's noise slid into silence. The bartender began to back away.

And the old devil rose up in Stark again. He didn't crave violence, but some dark part of him yearned for that most basic level of human competition that could be found only in combat. He felt the hard hilt of the bowie in his fist.

But another desire rose up in him as well. Prudence had all but accused him of deliberately picking fights with Barnett and the Sooner Kid for no other reason that to prove he was the better man. She hadn't been there to see him try to avoid killing the hapless robber in Ingalls. But she was here now to witness his reaction to this pointless challenge. His name hadn't entered into it, so there was no need to defend his reputation. There was nothing to be gained from killing this hombre, if he could avoid it.

"No deal," he said flatly. "I won the bet. Everybody here saw it. You try to kill me with that knife, I'll shoot you dead. And I promise you, I'm faster with a gun than I am with a knife." He let the words sink in, then added, "Maybe you ought to know who I am before you make up your mind. My name's James Stark. Some folks know me as the Peacemaker."

Maybe this time his reputation would prevent trouble.

The spirit went out of the knife artist, but the pride still lingered. "You will not match blades with me?" he challenged.

"I've already matched blades with you. It ain't worth either one of us dying over." Stark had given the man a clear out. No one could be faulted for being unwilling to match a knife against a gun in the hand of an expert.

"He's right, Roberto," an onlooker called.

"Peacemaker's bad medicine. Don't tangle with him!" another offered.

"I ain't betting on no killing!" one more voice joined in. "And somebody owes me ten bucks!"

The interest of the spectators turned toward collecting and paying off debts. The knife artist, Roberto, stood nonplussed.

"Keeping an eye on him," Stark collected Prudence and hustled Sorley out of the saloon.

Sorley dug in his heels once they were outside the bar. His eyes glinted suspiciously in the lantern light spilling onto the sidewalk through the grimy windows. "Can't say as how I'm not mighty obliged to you, Mister. But I'd like to hear about this business you mentioned before we go any further."

"The business is actually with me," Prudence spoke up.

Stark got the impression Sorley was seeing Prudence fully for the first time. The suspicion in his eyes turned to surprise, then to genuine interest. "Then I'm real flattered, ma'am. What can I do for you?"

Prudence ignored his amorous overtures and kept her tone businesslike. "I'm an attorney, Mr. Sorley, working for the family of Clarence Dunsmore. It seems you witnessed Mr. Dunsmore's will a short time back when you were staying at a roadhouse known as Rowland's. Do you recall those events?"

"Sure, I remember," Sorley admitted readily enough. "Ain't every day a body gets asked to witness a last will and testament."

"Well, Mr. Dunsmore has since passed away, and his will is being called into question. So I'm looking to verify his mental competency. Did you have any conversation with Mr. Dunsmore? I mean, did you talk with him enough to be certain that he knew what he was doing? As I understand it, the man had just been thrown from his horse on the trail."

"Yeah, that's what he told us. And he was bruised up a bit and walking kind of stiff, but he sounded okay to me."

"And you would be willing to testify to that in court?"

Sorley shrugged. "I guess so. I mean, we played a couple of hands of poker after we signed the will, and the old guy won both hands. You got to be right in the head to play poker so as to win, don't ya? I mean, especially against me. I sure wouldn't have any qualms about taking his money if he'd misplayed his cards. I am a professional, after all."

"Yeah," Stark said dryly, nodding back toward the saloon. "You're a real swift gambler, all right."

Prudence's glower silenced him. "Then you'll return with us to Earlsboro and testify on my clients' behalf that Mr. Dunsmore was in full command of his faculties when he executed his will?"

"Sure, I'll go with you," Sorley agreed. "The old man was as right as rain when he signed that will. It'll just take me a minute to get my horse out of the livery stable and check out of the hotel."

While they waited for Sorley to collect his things, Prudence smiled softly up at Stark. "I'm proud of you for not allowing that knife thrower to goad you into a fight."

"If you hadn't been there, I probably would've killed him," Stark grumbled in answer.

"Oh, hush!" Prudence slapped him on the shoulder. "You would have done no such thing, and you know it."

"Careful, that's my gun arm," he warned.

"Good!" She hit him again, this time with her fist.

"Ow!" He was still nursing his shoulder, much to Prudence's disgust, when Sorley reappeared. "Let's slope!" Stark said.

They made camp a few miles outside of town and hit the trail at sunup. Sorley was good company, relating tales of his adventures and misadventures. Prudence continued to probe for details about the signing of the will, and his story remained credible. Stark sensed she was satisfied Sorley would help their case.

The gambler seemed eager to cooperate and totally bedazzled by Prudence, which Stark could understand. Sorley also looked to be a bit puzzled about the relationship the two of them had. Stark could understand that, too.

Near midday, they rode into one of the rocky outcroppings of hills which studded the prairie like islands. Stark surveyed the rugged hillsides, but saw nothing to deter them from crossing. Reluctantly he led the way in. Riding around the hills would add a couple of hours to their trip.

He stayed alert as they threaded narrow draws and crossed small valleys, but even he had no warning.

A single shot tore the air, and Sorley flopped lifelessly from his saddle.

Chapter Nine

"**Y**ou reckon them two are going to make it back here with their witnesses?" Judge Horatio Hatch asked.

Thaddeus Jenkins considered the question carefully, as he always did with one put to him by the judge. Beneath the judge's irascible and disreputable appearance lurked a surprisingly keen and perceptive mind, well-steeped in legal theory and practice.

Still, after all these years Thaddeus had trouble predicting how Hatch would react to a given case. At times the judge's rulings were models of legal erudition, and at others they were the work of a temperamental child.

"Their time is now quite limited," he said in answer to the jurist's question. "But I believe they will be successful. They are both quite competent in their fields. Together they would make a formidable team."

The judge mulled Thaddeus's reply over. They were seated, as was their custom, at one of the tables in the saloon *cum* courtroom. Other than the two of them, the room was empty.

Hatch had a massive mug of beer in front of him, Thaddeus a bottle of ginger ale. Eyeing his beverage, Hatch shook his head. "Sure you don't want something stronger than that sweetened water?" he drawled.

"No, sir," Thaddeus answered as he always did. "I don't care for alcohol. My pa taught me a body who'd been drinking could never be sure if what he was doing was what *he* wanted or what the alcohol made him *think* he wanted. I prefer to make my decisions with a clear mind."

Hatch snorted scornfully to end the familiar exchange. Then he cocked his head. "It's a wonder them two ain't married."

"Not so much of a wonder," Thaddeus disagreed. "They are two awfully headstrong individuals. I imagine they disagree as much as they agree."

"Work well together, though."

"That they do."

"Did you know Stark from back before we hitched up?"

Thaddeus was often reticent about his past, although he felt no shame over any of it. If anything, he felt pride. He hadn't done too badly for the son of former slaves.

His parents had left him little in the way of material goods, but they had left a legacy which he considered of far greater value: their strong religious faith, and the belief that all men are created equal. They would be proud of him. He had worked jobs from saloon swamper to freight hauler to earn his way through law school, the only black man in his class. Coming West to practice law, he had picked up a few other skills as well, not the least of which was the ability to handle a six-gun better than most.

And he owed more than a little to the notorious Shotgun Judge, who unlike his judicial brethren, had been willing to look beyond the color of a man's skin to his abilities, and take him on as law clerk and bailiff.

Without undue pride he knew that the decision on Hatch's part had been a wise one. In return for his willingness to give a man a chance, the judge had obtained a skillful attorney and administrator with a shrewd legal mind.

After five years of unlikely partnership, the two men shared hard-forged bonds of mutual respect and loyalty toward each other.

"The Peacemaker and I handled a little trouble some time back," he answered the judge's question.

Hatch grunted and didn't press for details. "Hope him and that feisty little lady lawyer do make it back with their witnesses," he mused aloud. "I surely do hate to give that low-life Sooner Kid or whatever fool name he calls himself, title to a big chunk of his pa's holdings. I surely do."

Thaddeus maintained a judicious silence.

After a moment Hatch thrust his bearded jaw forward aggressively. "You disagree with me, do you?" he demanded.

Thaddeus steepled his fingertips then pressed his palms together. "I simply believe that in the absence of witnesses, the concept of equity might come into play under the circumstances of this case."

"No, by Godfrey!" Hatch's huge fist descended on the table and almost upended both mug and bottle. "You know better than that! This is not a case of the law, pure and simple! I have to decide, on the basis of the evidence presented, whether to allow a man to do what the law abhors, namely to disinherit a blood child."

Thaddeus didn't argue. Hatch had the law on his side, and they both knew it. Besides, no one could out-argue Hatch. When you persuaded him, it was by making your point and letting it germinate once the resulting tirade was finished.

But Thaddeus didn't think much of his chances here. It wasn't enough for a man to simply omit mention of a child in his will, thereby disinheriting his offspring. Under the ancient tradition of pretermitted heirship, the child had to be mentioned and pretty much specifically disinherited for it to stick. And even then, if the offspring could show that the maker of the will didn't have his full capacity, the will could be overturned.

Bringing in a doctor had been a shrewd maneuver for the attorney Grimes to pull. Eyewitnesses to the will, depending on their testimony, could overcome evidence like that, but it was still no easy row to hoe, even if the disinherited son was the spendthrift black sheep of the family.

Hatch drained the last of his beer, set the mug down with a thump, and glared sourly across the table as if to punctuate his outburst. "Keep an eye on things while I catch up on a few matters," he commanded. "Seen some strangers in town; don't like their looks. Could be they're in the traces with the Sooner Kid."

"Yessir." Thoughtfully Thaddeus watched Hatch lumber out of the room.

He was still thoughtful as he prowled the town in the afternoon sunlight. He, too, had seen a couple of strangers that that struck him as being more hard-bitten than even the rough crowd that usually frequented Earlsboro. The Kid had admitted on the stand to having what sounded like a gang back in the hills. Had some of them come down to partake of Earlsboro's pleasures?

Thaddeus completed a circuit of the town, nodding or speaking in return to greetings received from the citizens. As he began to retrace his path, he saw the Dunsmore girl and her Eastern beau, Fuller, emerge from the hotel some hundred yards distant along the dusty street.

Casually, her hand resting on his crooked arm, they began to stroll in the same direction Thaddeus himself was headed. They made a very fine-looking couple, he decided. He had noted them strolling thus on other days and had often exchanged pleasantries with them in passing.

The couple reached the end of the street, crossed over, and started back in his direction. Movement caught his attention, and he saw a man—one of the hardcase strangers—step out of a building the pair was nearing. He heard the mutter of voices, indistinct at this range, and something in their tones made his hackles rise.

Too fast for him to intervene, he then saw it all unfold like a cheap stage melodrama. The hardcase said something that made Donna Dunsmore react with shock and made

Fuller shoulder past her in obvious outrage to face her offender. Both men's voices were raised. Only a few words were spoken, but only a few were needed to spark trouble.

The hardcase made his draw, but Fuller got his gun out more quickly, snapping it clear of leather. His first bullet jolted his foe backward, spoiling the single shot the fellow got off. Fuller fired again, and his target started to fall.

Thaddeus lunged forward into a run, but was still able to clearly see the next act in the deadly play. A second figure stepped into view from an alley behind Fuller and the girl. The Sooner Kid stood poised, hands loose at his sides, fingers curled just a bit.

"Try me, Easterner!" his shrill voice carried.

Fuller wheeled, his gun already out and leveled. The Kid let him come full about, then stunningly still beat him to the shot. His right hand snaked across his belly to snatch out the pistol carried butt forward in the opposite holster. It spat a sharp tongue of flame, and Fuller was driven back against Donna. She tried to hold him upright, but couldn't support his weight as he collapsed. Coldly the Sooner Kid extended his six-gun toward his fallen victim.

Thaddeus jerked to a halt, his own pistol sweeping up from his holster. A setup, he was analyzing, in a detached part of his mind. The Kid had ruthlessly thrown his own man to the wolves to test Fuller and provide himself with a legally foolproof opportunity to finish the job if his underling failed. No jury would convict a man who pulled iron against an opponent with a gun already in his fist.

Thaddeus lined his pistol for aimed fire. He was too far distant to risk a snap shot, and he didn't want to kill if he could help it, particularly when the subject was a party in a case before the judge. In the heartbeat that the Kid took to savor his victory, Thaddeus fired. The Kid flinched as the unexpected bullet sent splinters flying from the nearest wall.

Thaddeus realigned his aim dead center on the Kid and yelled, "Hold it!" even as Dunsmore pivoted catlike his gun questing for his new target.

"Don't try it!" Thaddeus shouted. "I'm ready for you!" He stood motionless as a duelist out of the old days, arm extended at shoulder level. "Drop it!"

For a strained instant he thought the Kid would actually try to beat a second dead drop, then Dunsmore cautiously bent to place his pistol on the ground near his feet. His eyes never left Thaddeus. Decadent and dissipated the Sooner Kid might be, but Thaddeus no longer entertained the slightest doubt that he was a very dangerous man with a gun. Maybe the most dangerous he'd ever seen.

Thaddeus lowered his own pistol, but kept it leveled at waist height as he strode forward. A sickness rose in him at what he was afraid he might find. Had Dunsmore been successful in his ploy to eliminate one of the key protectors of his legal opponents?

He could only spare a glance as he drew near. The hapless hardcase was dead. Hurried, perhaps, by having to outshoot a man with a gun already drawn, the kid hadn't done as well. Thankfully, Fuller still lived. Half-sobbing, Donna was kneeling beside him, trying to tend his wound.

"Go get a doctor, girl!" Thaddeus said sharply. "Now!"

He wanted her clear of this, because he could tell the danger wasn't over yet.

Reluctantly she obeyed. Thaddeus kept his attention mostly on the Kid, but out of the edge of his vision he saw her hurry away in a flurry of skirts. He also saw that more gunslicks—strangers—seemed to have materialized out of the woodwork. Mingled with them was a scattering of recognizable patrons of the local saloons. Dishearteningly, none of them appeared particularly well-disposed toward him, Thaddeus noted. Just how many men could the Kid summon to do his bidding?

"You're outnumbered," the Kid commented in his whiskey hoarsened tones.

"My gun is trained on you alone," Thaddeus pointed out. "Clear everyone out of here so this man can get some help!" He saw the figures of the sycophantic Sab Tucker and the dapper Nash edging nearer to the side of their leader. "You two hold it!" he ordered.

They stopped, but Thaddeus didn't try to fool himself into believing he had control of the situation. He didn't— not by any stretch of the imagination.

He sensed movement among the men. Some of them were shifting so they would be behind him. And there was still the Kid's holstered right hand gun to worry about. . . .

"Nobody move, or I'll drill the Kid!" Thaddeus tried to gain some kind of hold on things.

The Kid grinned sardonically beneath his steerhorn mustache. "They can't clear out if you ain't going to let them move." There was no fear in him, Thaddeus saw. The Kid was enjoying the whole affair. He was eager to have a chance to pull his second gun.

And it looked like he was going to keep on pushing until he got that chance.

Thaddeus knew he must make his own move within the next handful of seconds. Whatever that move was going to be—

The stunning blast of the sawed-off shotgun and the eruption of the miniature crater in the hard-packed dirt of the street came at the same time.

"You're fixing to disturb the peace, and I plumb won't have it!" the familiar voice bellowed in tones that outdid even the report of the shotgun.

Striding like Colossus along the boardwalk, his pistol grip shotgun held negligently in one massive fist, Judge Horatio Hatch dominated the mob, the street, and pretty near the entire town in that moment.

Thaddeus felt a surge of hope. He was still in a dangerous position, but the odds in his favor had increased a great deal.

"Private quarrel, Judge," the Kid had enough brass to speak up. "No need for you to interfere."

The judge cast his gaze over the hard-bitten view. "Don't look too private to me," he drawled in stentorian tones. "I see a lot of unfamiliar faces."

"Just innocent bystanders," the Kid protested.

"Well, then it's time for them to stop standing by!" Hatch declared. "You fellows commence to vacating these premises or I'll have to begin locking you up for loitering. Now, there ain't much room in our hoosegow. It'll be plumb full once we get two or three of you in it. Then Thaddeus and me will just have to start killing the rest of you." He broke off and glared fiercely at the offenders. "There. That's my ruling, and I'm just the man who can enforce it."

The Kid scowled, then gave a resigned toss of his head. "You guys heard the judge. Clear out."

Thaddeus allowed himself a sigh of relief as the crowd began to disperse. For the first time he saw Sarah Dunsmore standing in a doorway behind Hatch, a rifle in her hand. She held it competently, too. The odds had been a little more even than he thought, which helped his heart rate return to normal a bit faster.

As the sidewalk cleared, Sarah dropped to her knees to cradle William Fuller's head in her lap. Donna had returned with the doctor by this time, and they all huddled over Fuller's fallen form.

Hatch lifted the sawed-off threateningly and stepped between the group and the Sooner Kid and his cronies, Nash and Tucker, who still loitered a short distance down the sidewalk.

The Kid smirked and backed away, his hands raised defensively. "The Eastern dude drew first, Judge. Just ask your bailiff there. There was plenty of others saw it, too."

"Go ahead and get out of here," Hatch snarled. "And there better not be no more shootings in my town that can be linked up to you, or I'll let this Greener hand down the sentence in this case."

The Kid smiled indolently and sauntered away down the sidewalk with the others following.

Thaddeus turned to the doctor. "How's Mr. Fuller doing, Doc?"

"He's alive, that's about all I can say at the moment. Will you help me carry him over to the hotel, Mr. Jenkins? I'll try to get the bullet out there."

Thaddeus nodded and holstered his gun. The Eastern constable didn't look at all good, he thought to himself. In fact, there was nothing good about any aspect of the situation brewing in this town.

He offered up a fervent prayer for the safe return of the Peacemaker and his lady with their witnesses.

Chapter Ten

"Are you okay?" Stark asked sharply.

"You're crushing me!" Prudence gasped. "Move!" She then gave a little cry when a bullet chipped fragments of stone inches above their heads before screaming off in a ricochet.

Keeping his head down, Stark rolled from atop her. Even as Sorley was falling, he had snatched his sporting rifle from its scabbard, and reached to encircle Prudence's slender waist with one long arm where she rode beside him. Kicking free of his stirrups, he took her tumbling with him from their saddles and into the shelter of a rocky draw. A second shot had whipcracked past them as they fell.

Shifting now, he brought his rifle awkwardly into position and gazed up at the rugged hillside opposite their refuge. A telltale cloud of smoke hung there. Still half-

129

sprawled, he levered the big Winchester, snugged the butt to his shoulder, sighted just below the smoke, and returned fire. The long-barreled sporting rifle had all the power of an old-time buffalo gun. Three times he fired, the heavy slugs cracking and scarring the rocks where he calculated the sharpshooter was hiding.

Instantly Stark flattened himself. "Keep down!" he snapped needlessly to Prudence. "Count his shots!"

She raised her wide-eyed face. "What?"

"Count the number of shots! There've been three from him so far."

Any further questioning of his orders was cut off as the fusillade began in a frenzied flurry of rifle fire. Bullet after bullet went keening off the sheltering stone or kicked dirt from the bank behind them.

"My heavens! How many of them are up there?" Prudence exclaimed.

"Just one."

"How does he reload so fast?"

"He doesn't need to," Stark growled. Then as the shooting stopped abruptly he added, "I make it twenty. What about you?"

"I—I lost count."

Stark glowered, then gritted his teeth as he reared up to return fire again. It was almost his undoing. The sharpshooter had been waiting for him. Another handful of shots were flung at him as fast as a top-notch rifleman could operate a rapid-fire repeater.

Stark ducked frantically back. He had a plan—or maybe nothing more than a gamble born of a wish and a prayer.

Everything was riding on how well he'd figured the shifty workings of a sniper's mind. But no scheme in creation would help him if he let himself get nailed before he ever had a chance to play his desperate hand.

The barrage of shots came to a halt. Stark tallied the total at twenty-six. He took stock. Sorley lay unmoving where he had fallen. He'd been dead by the time he hit the ground, Stark calculated. The horses had high-tailed it, but he knew Red, his sorrel stallion, wouldn't stray far.

"I can keep this up all day, Stark!" a voice rang out from the rocky face of the hill. "How many rounds does that cannon of yours hold? Six? Eight?"

"Enough to take you down, Talon!" Stark hollered in reply.

For he had no doubts but that it was Lute Talon up there in those rocks with his Evans rifle. The feral hunter had been dogging their trail at least since Bass Barnett's brutal attempt at murder in the wrestling ring.

And Stark was equally certain that it was the Sooner Kid who'd dispatched Talon on his bloody mission.

"Won't do you no good even if you manage to weasel out of this," the hunter's mocking tones echoed down at them. "When you left Ingersoll, I circled back and put a brace of slugs in that fool wrestler. Now with the tinhorn dead, you and the lady lawyer got no witnesses at all!"

Beside Stark, Prudence lowered her head and moaned in despair.

Stark felt the pressing weight of their failure himself. But the trial wasn't going to matter much to him or Prudence if they didn't get out of this fix alive.

He lined the rifle and sent another heavy caliber messenger up at the sniper's position.

Seemed like he came close, because Talon opened up again with a vengeance. Grimly Stark counted the shots as they came. Some of them were fired so close together that their reports almost merged.

"Thirty-two," Stark counted tautly, and sent up a silent prayer. "Thirty-three!"

Stark let his heart beat once before he moved. Talon would likely be expecting him to break from cover, maybe try to reach the hill. If Stark had figured it right, Talon believed that he, Stark, thought the Evans rifle was empty.

Stark heard Prudence's startled cry as he surged to his feet with the Sporting Rifle already lined to fire. His sights came center on the unmistakable buckskinned figure of Talon a hundred yards distant, likewise bringing his rifle to bear. As Stark had hoped—prayed—the hunter had risked showing himself to get a clear shot with his last bullet—the thirty-fourth—at what he expected to be an exposed moving target.

Talon was quick enough to see his mistake and try to get his motionless target in his sights. Stark had the fleeting impression of staring down the barrel of the Evans rifle as it came to bear.

Then he shot Talon dead center in the chest.

The boom of the sporting rifle bounced away off the hills. Talon reeled, and Stark, ratcheting the lever in a blur, had time to get in one more shot before the hunter dropped from sight.

Stark lowered the smoking rifle. Automatically he

thumbed shells from his bandolier into its breech as he scanned the surrounding terrain. He saw nothing to fret about. Talon had worked alone.

"How did you know what he'd do?" Puzzlement was in Prudence's voice. She was dusting herself off as she gazed up at Stark.

"I didn't know," he answered, "not for sure." He fell silent, then went on almost absently. "Talon and I crossed trails back in Earlsboro. Knowing his breed, I suspected he might be riding for the Kid. So I misled him into thinking I didn't know how many shells his rifle held, figuring it might give me an edge if I ever had to go up against him. Turns out I was right."

Prudence had stopped brushing at herself in mid-motion. "You were figuring out how to kill him from the moment you met him?" she asked in disbelief.

Stark looked away from her. "He was doing the same with me."

Prudence let her hands fall limply to her sides. Her trim shoulders slumped. "Sometimes I hate it that you're so good at what you do."

Stark stared at the spot where Talon had disappeared. "My being good at this didn't help much in bringing the witnesses back, did it?" he said bitterly. Rifle in hand he trudged toward the rocky hill. He heard a single strangled sound from behind him.

He used some caution in approaching Talon's perch. He bypassed one of the beartraps set to clamp shut on the ankle of anyone seeking to steal up on the hunter. Talon had been a cautious man himself.

The hunter still bore a look of surprise where he sprawled on a ledge beneath an overhang. It was the last expression he'd ever bear.

Stark stood over him for a spell, thinking of Prudence waiting below. He knew she'd spoke out of the depths of her despair over the ugly turn things had taken, but her words had still cut at him. The judge had talked of legacies. What kind of legacy was he going to leave? One of death and violence dealt out in the name of righteous causes? It seemed a sorry estate to mark his passing.

Somewhere further up the hill a mule brayed. Must be Talon's beast, Stark thought. He'd wasted enough time brooding over a dead man who, under just about any calculation, deserved the death he'd gotten.

Bending, Stark picked up the Evans rifle lying beside Talon's outstretched hand. He looked up toward where the mule had brayed and saw heavy storm clouds beginning to build overhead. Autumn storms could be stemwinders. He'd best get to the chores at hand.

He managed, with some sweet talk, to edge close enough to the cantankerous mule to divest it of its burdens and loose it from its tether so it could fend for itself. Returning to Talon, he dumped the body unceremoniously in a crevice and piled rocks atop it. He didn't think a cross was needed in view of where Talon had most likely ended up.

Dark clouds brooded in the sky at dusk, and the wind howled cold and barren out of the west as Stark looked for a campsite where they could last out a stormy night. Prudence's mare had followed Red's lead and stopped without running off very far from the fracas just passed, so they'd resumed their journey with little wasted time after burying Sorley.

Prudence spoke little, lifting her head only to glance apprehensively at the lowering clouds from time to time. The failure of their mission obviously set heavily on her bowed shoulders.

Cover was hard to find on the wind-swept prairie. Gullies and draws could turn into raging torrents from runoff after a rain, and stands of trees were few and far between. At last Stark reined up on a grassy stretch just below the crest of a ridge. It would serve to break the wind. He wasn't feeling any too chipper himself.

"This will do."

Prudence didn't argue or comment, but fell to fixing a simple meal as Stark made camp. Darkness came quickly as the clouds swallowed the sun. They ate swiftly and in silence, then began cleaning and stowing away the few utensils they'd used.

Finally Prudence straightened and looked up at him. "Jim, I'm sorry about what I said back there," she spoke softly.

Stark hitched his shoulders. "You weren't that far out of line. Sometimes I'm not too happy myself about some of my skills."

Her eyes grew wide. "Most of the time you act as though you never have any doubts about anything you do."

"Most of the time I don't. I just look on it as doing what I must to survive."

"And to help others survive," she acknowledged quietly.

"If Talon had killed you, I'd have been next. I . . . I didn't even thank you for saving my life."

"No need," he said roughly.

"Yes, there is a need," she insisted. "You're always bailing me out of one scrape or another, and I'm never grateful enough. Why do you continue to put up with me?"

He almost smiled. "Kinda gotten used to you always probing into my motives. Keeps me thinking. Keeps me honest with myself. . . ."

"And with others," she said firmly. "I've never met a more honest person." She lowered her gaze, then lifted it to his face. When she spoke her tone was almost a whisper. "Maybe that's why I—" She broke off and seemed to fumble for words. "Why I—I trust you so," she managed at last.

Stark met her gaze, thought he'd never seen anything so beguiling as her dark eyes.

"I trust you, too," he said hoarsely. "There's nobody I'd rather have siding me in a fracas than you."

Her dark eyes sparkled brighter. "You're joking, right?"

"No joke. Nobody I'd rather ride a rough trail with. We make a great team."

She caught his gaze and held it. "Yes, we do," she whispered. "A great team . . ."

The air between them seemed to tremble. Then a blinding flash of lightning knifed to the ground in the distance, and a blast of sound rocked them. Prudence gave a soft cry and somehow suddenly she was clinging to him, and he held her tightly. Neither of them moved. The static charge left by the lightning bolt faded slowly.

Prudence laughed in embarrassment. "Sorry," she said breathlessly. "The noise just startled me so."

Another strike, even closer, made her bury her face in his shoulder. Stark tightened his embrace protectively. "The storm's gonna be a doozy," he ventured in a strained voice.

"Yes." She raised her face and forced a smile. "Sorry again. I guess my nerves are frayed, what with all that gunfire earlier, and now this. . . . Still want this cringing coward siding you in a fracas?"

He looked down on her. "Anytime. Anywhere." All at once he couldn't resist lowering his lips to claim her trembling ones. And she didn't object. He had wanted to kiss her many times before, but had always feared her reaction. But this time it all seemed so right. . . .

Only the elements were in disagreement. Angry raindrops began to pelt them as another blinding flash split the air. Prudence broke off the kiss and pushed against him. "Jim, we need to get in out of this."

"You're right." His breath was coming raggedly. "You'd better get in the tent."

The wind plucked at her dark hair. "What about you?"

"I've got my slicker and a tarp to pull over me. I'll be fine out here."

It was clear she wanted to argue with him, but then thought better of it. He became aware that she was shaking. He quickly released her, and she brushed past him to duck into her tent. She dropped the flap, and a moment later a lantern's dim glow shone through the heavy fabric.

It suddenly dawned on him that he was feeling a bit shaky himself. He surmised that neither one of them was prepared for what had just happened. It was a lot to ponder and sort out—that is, if it could be sorted out. But maybe it would serve to take his mind off the rough night he was facing. He did his best to get comfortable as the wind whipped over the crest of the hill and swept down on him, carrying with it the first driving rush of rain. The lightning marched ever closer.

"Jim." Prudence had her head stuck out of the flap. "You'll catch your death of cold if you stay out there! We can share the tent." He was relieved to hear her voice was back to normal.

"Not a good idea," he insisted.

"I won't bite."

"I might," Stark growled, hoping to regain some of their former easy-going comraderie.

Prudence apparently wanted that, too. "I'll risk it," she shot back.

The rain pelted him harder. He could sense the approach of an advancing waterfall just beyond the crest. Lightning shook the ground and the thunderclap made his ears ring. Prudence was getting soaked. Her dark sodden hair framed her face.

"Jim, don't be a fool!" she cried.

Stark relented. In another moment he guessed she would come out to try and drag him to shelter. He shed the tarp, and she drew back to let him enter. He was immediately aware of the feminine warmth of her nearness and the comforting shelter of the tent.

She wore a thick cotton gown, buttoned at the neck, but

the sight of her in the glow of the lantern made his throat go tight once again.

He struggled out of his slicker as she dried her hair and wrapped a blanket about herself before settling crosslegged across from him. For a few moments they sat in a breathless silence, their knees almost touching, listening to the elements beseige the tent.

The ground bucked beneath the tent, and a blinding flash illuminated the darkness outside. The lantern flame shrank to a point of light.

Prudence gave a soft cry and ducked her head. Stark thought—hoped—she might come back into his arms, but she only hugged herself tighter. He was more than ever conscious of the softness of the cotton gown, the sweet scent of her, and the outline of her slender form through the homespun fabric.

Neither of them moved as their eyes met and held again. Stark watched the fear flow from her to be replaced by a different sort of tension.

Prudence pulled the blanket more securely about herself. "Thank you," she said quietly, "for not pushing matters any further tonight." Then a gamine grin touched her lips. "I think."

Stark's own lips quirked. "Just don't try to take advantage of me now that you've lured me into this compromising situation."

"I think you'll be safe as long as you stay on your side of the tent."

"I'm not so sure. After all, who came rushing into whose arms out there?"

Prudence sniffed. "There were extenuating circumstances."

Stark rolled his slicker lengthwise and put it between them. "There," he announced. "Now we should be safe from each other. I hope you don't snore."

"Jim! How dare you say such a thing!"

Stark extinguished the lantern before she could see the smile that spread across his face at her indignation. "Good night, Miss McKay," he said into the darkness.

"I'll have you know I do not snore! Good night!"

Stark stretched out on his side of the blanket, arm pillowing his head. The storm's fury seemed to have slackened. The sound of the rain, and the sense of her nearness lulled him into an easy slumber.

He awoke near dawn and realized that sometime in the night both of them had moved. The wadded slicker was by his feet, and Prudence, still wrapped in her blanket, was snuggled against him fast asleep.

Gingerly Stark propped himself up on an elbow and stared down at her face in the dim light. He wasn't thinking of much of anything except that it was mighty nice to be here beside her.

Dangerous thoughts for a troubleshooter used to riding a lone trail.

He might've shifted, or maybe she sensed his gaze on her. For she stirred, then opened her eyes and looked sleepily up at him. For a couple of heartbeats she seemed perfectly content.

"Good morning, Miss McKay," he said wryly.

She went rigid, realized the impropriety of their positions, and moved hastily away, drawing her blanket up defensively.

"Hold it," he said before she could speak. "There were extenuating circumstances."

"Such as?" she questioned warily.

"Well, you were snoring, and I was trying to—"

She kicked hard at him. "Get out of my tent! I should've left you out in the rain!"

"That's the story of my life," he groused, as he reached to get his hat and slicker. "I'm always getting thrown out when the sun comes up!"

"With good cause!" She got in another kick from where she sat before he made it out of the tent. Behind him he fancied he heard stifled laughter.

But the lighthearted mood quickly slipped from both of them as they made ready to ride out. Looking far off across the grasslands, Stark thought of Judge Hatch and his makeshift courtroom awaiting them. There wasn't much to be lighthearted about.

"I should've known the other side would bring a doctor in to testify," Prudence scolded herself. She seemed to have been following the same trail with her thoughts. "I should have—" She broke off abruptly as if some new notion had come to her. "Oh, good grief!" she exclaimed. "How could I have overlooked something so obvious!"

Stark stared at her in puzzlement. "What in tarnation—"
Then he, too, stopped short as he somehow caught the

drift of her thoughts. "It might do the trick," he said. "But we'll have to use the spurs to get there in time."

"It simply must work!" Prudence insisted, then implored, "Dear, Lord, please let it work!"

Chapter Eleven

"This court is now in session," Thaddeus Jenkins intoned. "The honorable Horatio Hatch presiding."

The door to the side room where he waited was slightly ajar so Stark could see a good slice of the makeshift courtroom. The Sooner Kid was present with his cronies, Sab Tucker and Nash. All of them were seated at one of the lawyers' tables. The Kid's dissolute features were set in an ugly sneer. Beside him, the sycophantic Tucker seemed to be chuckling silently, glancing frequently at his boss as though seeking approval. The nattily-dressed Nash had a contemptuous lift to his thin lips. For his part, Attorney Lance Grimes exuded a supercilious, oily confidence.

Those boys looked mighty sure of themselves, Stark thought with a bleak grin.

Prudence McKay appeared prim and very professional in

a decorous ladies suit. The past few days and weeks of hard travel didn't show on her. Stark had a moment's disturbing recollection of her in a cotton gown snuggled close against him. He shook the impression off. He needed his wits about him.

Prudence's clients—mother, Sarah, and daughter, Donna— sat composed and motionless, except for the solicitous looks Donna kept directing at William Fuller, who sat beside her. The New York constable was pale and drawn, but he was getting about well enough considering the wound he had taken. He'd had a touch of divine intervention, Stark reflected. The Kid wasn't known for leaving hombres who'd faced him with a gun able to walk around.

Presiding over this unusual assemblage, the Shotgun Judge glowered indiscriminantly at those present, not sparing the townsfolk who had come to see the show.

The pistol grip of the shotgun crashed down on the tabletop. "Order!" Hatch bellowed, although every person in the room had already fallen silent.

As usual Hatch skipped any further preliminaries. "You got any of them witnesses to the will, Counselor McKay?" he demanded. "Don't see nobody I don't recognize here."

Prudence had risen to her feet the moment he addressed her. "No, Your Honor, I do not have any of the witnesses present, for reasons which should become clear shortly. However," she forestalled any comment from Hatch, "I do have another witness I'd like to place on the stand, with your permission."

"Your Honor, I see no need for any further testimony in this matter," Lance Grimes spoke up. "Since she has failed to produce the witnesses as ordered, the Court should rule in favor of my client and have the so-called will thrown out."

"I don't recall asking you to butt in, shyster," Hatch growled. "And I sure ain't in need of you telling me when or how to make my rulings. Now, you just sit yourself down!"

His face flushing scarlet, Grimes sat.

Hatch glowered inquiringly at Prudence. "Well, proceed. Who is this proposed witness?"

"Judge, I've chosen to hold my witness incognito out of concern for his safety. Mr. Dunsmore elected to send a hired killer to eliminate all the witnesses who signed the will. Unfortunately, the killer was successful in this enterprise, but his success cost him his life. My colleague, James Stark, will be able to confirm this with his testimony."

The pounding butt of the shotgun stilled the clamor which arose at her announcement. Grimes was sputtering about relevance and hearsay. The Kid and his cronies had gone into a sudden huddle. The spectators were murmuring excitedly.

"Is Jim Stark your witness, Miss McKay?" Hatch demanded when the uproar subsided.

"No, Your Honor," Prudence declared. "My witness is Dr. Robert Henderson, who was Clarence Dunsmore's family physician."

Stark turned to his companion. "You're on, Doc."

The physician was a short, stocky man with a face lined from years of dealing with human hurt and misery. He nodded shortly and stepped past Stark to enter the courtroom.

Stark eased through the doorway behind him and positioned himself, shoulders against the wall, where he had a clear view of the Kid and his cohorts. He met the Kid's fierce glare impassively.

Grimes was complaining about a lack of relevance and his failure to receive prior notice of Henderson's appearance as a witness.

Hatch cut him off. "You pulled the same stunt on the lady, and I let it ride, Counselor. Turnabout's fair play. I'll hear the witness." He actually looked to be pleased with this development.

Dr. Henderson took the stand. In short order Prudence handled the preliminaries. Yes, he had a medical degree from a reputable medical school. Yes, he had practiced medicine on the frontier for some thirty years now. He had experience treating every type of injury or malady common to frontier life. For the last several years his practice had been located in Shawnee. And, yes, he had known Clarence Dunsmore.

"Was he a patient of yours?"

"Yes, he was. And I counted him as a friend."

"In your capacity as friend or physician, did you ever know him to be incompetent to make decisions for himself?"

"No, I did not. He always knew exactly what he wanted to do. Once he made up his mind, it would've taken a stampede of longhorns to change it. And even that might not do it."

Some of the onlookers chuckled, and Stark saw several

of them nodding agreement. Grimes fumed, but after a glance at the judge, kept his seat.

"Were you aware of the relationship he had with his son?" Prudence went on.

"What relationship?" Henderson scoffed. "It near broke his heart the way that boy turned out to be a villain and a spendthrift."

Stark kept his eyes on the villainous spendthrift. The Kid's face was seared with a lethal rage. He looked capable of killing and of doing a good job of it. Stark was grateful for the hideout .38 nestled comfortably under his coat.

The Kid and his pards weren't showing any iron, but Stark reckoned they hadn't abided by the judge's prohibition on guns in the courtroom any more than he had.

"I've told you the date of Mr. Dunsmore's will, have I not, Dr. Henderson?" Prudence pressed.

"Yep, but I already knew the date."

"And how is it that you knew?"

"Because Clarence himself told me about it the next day when he had me give him a checkup."

Stark grinned tightly at the Kid. At his first meeting with the widow and her daughter, the older woman had told of her husband's trip to a doctor after his mishap. Once Prudence had recalled that fact, it hadn't been too hard to locate the particular physician and enlist him to their cause, although time had been running short.

As Clarence Dunsmore's regular physician, who had examined him within twenty-four hours of his having made out his will, Henderson's testimony trumped anything that

Grimes' bought doctor could offer. It was the kind of testimony that could make or break a will contest.

"And when you examined Mr. Dunsmore on that occasion did you discuss his family with him?"

"Sure did. He told me about the will and how he was planning to have things divvied up after his death."

"And did he specifically mention his wife and his two children?"

"He sure did."

"So," Prudence ticked off the points, "he knew the natural objects of his bounty and understood the nature of the will he had prepared and signed. Is that your testimony?"

"Yes, ma'am, it is."

"And do you believe in your professional opinion that he knew the full extent of the assets that he owned at the time?"

"I do. I don't reckon there was ever a day of his adult life when Clarence Dunsmore didn't know every acre of land he owned, every head of livestock he had on it, and every penny he had in the bank."

Deftly, Prudence had extracted the three key points in determining capacity to sign a will, Stark noted proudly.

"Was there any indication that he was being influenced by any other person?"

Henderson actually smiled with amusement. "Clarence wasn't a man prone to being influenced to do anything he didn't want to do. He was stubborn as all get-out."

"Ain't that the truth?" one of the spectators stage-whispered with feeling, and drew an assortment of chuckles.

"Enough of that!" the judge warned.

Prudence had closed the final avenue of attack. "No further questions, Your Honor," she said.

"Your witness, Grimes," Hatch rumbled.

Grimes was clearly shaken by the turn the hearing had taken. But he tried his best.

It was to no avail. Emphatically, Henderson restated all the key points he had made. The cross-examination began to come apart like a tar paper shack caught in a twister. Sweat poured from Grimes, and with it went the smug air of confidence that had clung to him during the earlier proceedings.

"Why are you here, Doctor?" Grimes demanded at last. "Are you being paid for your testimony? Are you for hire?"

Henderson bristled. "I'm not getting paid a wooden nickel to be here, sir. I'm testifying in honor of Clarence Dunsmore, who was a friend and patient of mine. I'd wager that makes my motives a sight cleaner than your own. How much are you getting paid to represent the Sooner Kid?"

"He's got you there, Counselor," Hatch butted in before Grimes could finish sputtering his outrage. "And I reckon I've heard enough to make my ruling."

"Your Honor," Grimes managed to protest, "I have a closing argument, and I would like leave to seek further witnesses—"

"Wouldn't do no good. I've already made up my mind. Now quit yapping and listen to my ruling." Hatch paused and swung his haggy head back and forth to rake his gaze across the courtroom. "I'll have Thaddeus write this all up proper so I can sign it," he advised the attorneys.

Then he drew a deep breath and spoke. "My ruling in this here matter is that the will is valid; that Clarence Dunsmore was of sound mind when he wrote and signed it; and that it serves to pass his entire estate according to its terms."

Stark saw the wild rage flare even hotter in the Kid's face, and he pushed himself away from the wall to stand wary and alert, hand ready to dart for the .38. The dapper Nash spotted his movement and hastily whispered something to his boss.

For a moment the Kid reminded Stark of a fighting dog straining to get into the pit. His full attention was on the judge.

Hatch was aware of the Kid's lethal glare. His voice rumbled ominously, "You plan to appeal this matter right now, Mr. Dunsmore?" He sat like a barbarian king on a throne with the pistol grip sawed-off shotgun at his scepter. "Personally, I'd advise against it."

Nash gripped the Kid's shoulder with taloned fingers and spoke even more urgently to him. The Kid's head moved a notch to eye Stark. Out of the edge of his vision, Stark saw that Thaddeus Jenkins had risen from his table and stood in a casual loose-jointed stance that somehow had a deadly potential to it. Likewise, William Fuller was just easing to his feet.

Stark guessed he wasn't the only one who'd disregarded Hatch's rules about guns at this rodeo.

Nash muttered something further to the Kid, and the outlaw's glare shifted balefully to his stepmother and half-sister. By degrees, like a rattler deciding not to strike, he relaxed with a final frustrated shake of his shaggy head.

"That's better, Mr. Dunsmore," Hatch admonished. "Now I reckon it's only fair to warn you that, based on what I've heard here today, I will have a warrant sworn out for your arrest on suspicion of hiring murder to be done. It's my best advice that you skedaddle out of this Territory and not let me catch you here again. Otherwise, I'll personally serve that warrant. Understand?"

The Kid looked away from the women long enough to nod grudgingly in the judge's direction. "I savvy," he growled. "Come on, boys, let's hightail it out of this kangaroo court."

Tucker and Nash followed close on his heels as he stalked from the chamber. Grimes looked stricken. He hesitated, then scurried after them. "Just a minute, Mr. Dunsmore," he called. "About my fee—"

Stark wouldn't have bet much on Grimes collecting even a cent as the quartet disappeared out the door.

"Court dismissed!" Hatch boomed.

In the hubbub that arose, Stark wended his way across the room until he could peer out the window. The Kid and his crew had already disappeared, leaving only a billowing cloud of dust hanging in the street.

He became aware of movement beside him, and Prudence almost danced over to stand in front of him. Her dark eyes were sparkling. A smile wreathed her piquant features. "We did it! We won!" she enthused and hugged him tightly.

"Congratulations, Counselor." He dropped one big hand on her shoulder and squeezed briefly.

She drew back, gazing intently up into his face. "We won!" she repeated, but some of her vivacious air had slipped away.

"I know," Stark said, "and you deserve all the credit. You did a masterful job of presenting your surprise witness. Grimes didn't stand a chance against you. So . . . I figure my job's over now."

"What do you mean?" she asked suspiciously.

"You hired me to protect your clients until the will was admitted to probate. That's happened. Now I've got some other pressing business that needs tending to."

She stepped away from him. "You're going after them, aren't you?" she accused sharply.

Stark shrugged. "Recon so."

"I can't believe you're going back on your word like this! You specifically promised me—"

Stark brought up a hand to forestall her words. "Now, don't misstate our deal. I promised not to pick a fight with the Kid until the job you hired me to do was finished. I kept my promise. I'm on my own now. Neither you nor anybody else is pulling my reins."

"That doesn't give you any right to hunt Blake Dunsmore down and kill him! Or worse, get killed yourself!"

"I'm not planning on doing either one," Stark said gruffly. "And I make my living tracking men down, remember? You're the one who discovered Dunsmore's wanted in Kansas. Besides, you heard the judge say he'll issue a warrant for the Kid's arrest. He's a dangerous fugitive—wanted in at least two states. That gives me all the right I need."

"You're not fooling anyone! You're just doing it to prove you're better with a gun than he is!" Prudence shot back angrily.

"I'm doing it to protect your clients. *And you!*" Stark countered harshly. "You saw the way he looked at those women. You know as well as I do he'll be coming after them. And you, too, if you get in his path. Think about it! Remember who gets the estate if they're both dead! That's my reason for going after him."

"But that's not your only reason," she persisted.

Stark hesitated only a heartbeat. "It's my main reason."

Prudence stamped her foot. "Jim, I don't want you to go! I won't have you taking foolish chances and risking your life like this. You'll be taking on his whole gang!"

"I don't work for you anymore. You can't tell me what to do."

Wheeling, he strode to the door and stalked out.

Chapter Twelve

He was certain he'd struck their trail when he spotted where three riders cut off from the heavily travelled road and headed into the wild country to the north. They were moving at a good clip, and Stark blunted the edge of eagerness spurring him to greater speed.

Rugged hills, wooded patches, and deep draws made it easy enough for a man to ride into a bushwhacking without hurrying to meet the event. He kept Red, his big sorrel stallion, to an easy gait.

He had no doubts his hunch was right. The Kid wouldn't be satisfied leaving well enough alone. He'd be fuming over his defeat in court, spoiling for revenge, and eaten up with greed. It had clearly been Nash who'd advised him to bide his time and eliminate the other heirs, although the

Kid himself would've thought of it eventually. The Kid clearly had to be dealt with once and for all.

Abruptly he felt Red's pace slow. The stallion tossed his head and snorted with alarm. Stark drew up sharp on the reins, and the rifle bullet fired from the nearby hillside whined past his face with a slap of disturbed air.

There was no cover. He was caught in the open. Only Red's sensing of the ambusher's presence or, more likely that of his horse, had stopped Stark from catching a bullet.

No place to run except right at the hidden marksman.

He had about a second's time. In it he swung Red about, lifted the reins to clamp his teeth shut on them, and plucked the lever-action shotgun from its scabbard. As he snapped the butt to his shoulder, he kicked the stallion into a snaking charge toward the hill. There was no aiming of the shotgun, there was only levering and firing in the general direction of the bushwhacker's position. He kept his knees clamped tight to Red's surging body.

Back and forth he zig-zagged up the hill, pumping alternating rounds of buckshot and solid slugs in a barrage of screaming lead.

Under that withering firepower, and faced by Stark's barbaric charge into the teeth of a rifle, the drygulcher was overwhelmed. As the shotgun ran dry, Stark slewed Red around a rocky outcropping, scarred by buckshot and slugs, and threw down with a cocked .45 on the man cowering there.

Then he snorted derisively. "You're a mighty poor

shakes as a bushwhacker, Tucker. And I'm getting mighty tired of folks trying to ambush me."

Tucker stared up at the assortment of saddle guns in Stark's gear. "You really did it, didn't you?" he gulped. "You killed Talon."

"That's generally the way I treat drygulchers." Stark stepped down from Red.

Tucker scooted himself backwards until his shoulders fetched up against the outcropping which had sheltered him. "Don't kill me, Peacemaker."

Stark wagged his head. "You're a gutless wonder, Tucker, a bully and a coward. You ain't worth killing. That is, if you help me out."

"What do you want? I'll do anything!"

"Where's the Kid?"

"He had his men waiting up here for him. He left me to watch his backtrail. He's taking the rest of them to Earlsboro to root out his half-sister and that widow woman. They're circling around so as to come into town from the opposite direction from what we rode out. The Kid thought nobody'd be expecting an attack from that end of town."

Stark felt the touch of an icy serpent on his nape. "Men?" he demanded. "How many?"

"Twenty. Twenty-five. Maybe more. We had some fellows from town join up with us after he gunned down that Eastern dude."

Stark set his jaw. The Kid had a small army at his command. He glared down at Tucker. His nostrils flared and his shoulders expanded. He raised the .45 threateningly.

"Don't do it, Peacemaker! I didn't want no part of it, I swear!"

"Ride out of the territories and never come back," Stark rasped coldly. "If I ever see you again, I'll drop you with whatever's to hand—gun, knife, fist, or boot."

Tucker nodded frantically. "Yeah. Sure. I understand. You won't see me in these parts again!" He half-ran, half-scrambled toward his horse tethered nearby.

Stark wouldn't turn his back on him. He watched until Tucker was astride his saddle and spurring his horse up the grade before he climbed aboard Red.

"The Kid will take you, Peacemaker!" Tucker's braying tones echoed. "You can't beat him."

"We'll soon see," Stark muttered, and put Red down the hill almost as recklessly as they'd come up it.

Urgency throbbed in his blood. He'd been right in figuring the Kid's next move, but it had come far faster than he'd reckoned. The Kid was riding against his own kin with a pack of ruthless killers that almost certainly numbered among them those who bore a grudge against Hatch and likely even Thaddeus Jenkins.

They had a lead on him, but they were swinging wide to come in from an unexpected direction. Maybe, Stark calculated, he could beat them there in time to give warning.

As he came off the hill, he heeled Red into a run and offered up a prayer that he'd be in time.

Red responded with the unbroken spirit of a mustang. Stark leaned low over the saddle and let him have his head. A deep draw flashed beneath as Red hurtled it with a surging leap that needed no coaxing from his rider. Then with a touch of the reins they were skirting the looming mass of rocky hillside and racing pell-mell through a stand of cottonwood trees. The low hanging branches struck like miniature whips at man and beast alike.

When they came out on the road, Red was blowing, and patches of sweat turned his rusty coat black. Stark eased him a trifle, but Red wasn't having it. He was doing what instinct, spirit, and training drove him to do. He ran like a norther blowing down from Kansas as they raced along the road back into Earlsboro.

But all his effort wasn't enough, Stark realized as they reached the edge of town. There was no activity, barely any sign of life. Stark saw a pale face vanishing from a window behind a hastily dropped curtain.

Trouble was brewing, sure enough. The townsfolk knew it and had ducked for cover.

Stark pulled the shotgun from its scabbard and eased Red forward at a walk. His eyes flicked back and forth, and more than once he spared a glance over his shoulder. The Kid might've dispatched a lookout to this end of town.

From up ahead came a growing murmur born of numerous men sitting their restless mounts. Stark eased Red over to the shadowed side of the street. He kept the shotgun's barrel pointed upward, ready to be tilted down with a twitch of his wrist.

The murmur grew louder, and the sound of individual voices reached his ears. He dismounted and catfooted forward, leaving Red ground-hitched. From the cover of an alley, he peered out at the scene in front of the judge's converted saloon.

Tucker hadn't exaggerated. In front of a pack of near thirty human lobos, the Sooner Kid carried on a shouted conversation with someone inside the courthouse.

"You hear me, Judge? I know all of you are in there. This can end real easy. Just send the womenfolk out, and we'll go away peaceable. And that includes that snippy lady lawyer. And better throw in the Eastern constable, too. I don't want him on my backtrail. I'll finish what I started with him."

The Kid had them all cornered. Likely he had men all around the building, Stark surmised.

"I'm waiting, Judge!"

"First man what makes a move on my courthouse, and I'll blow you out of the saddle!" Hatch's unmistakable bellow responded at last.

"I got guns trained on every window, with orders to shoot at any sign of movement!" the Kid retorted. "You won't get the chance to blow me or anybody else out of the saddle."

Stark noted several horsemen scattered about with rifles levelled on the building. This was a powderkeg waiting to explode.

And the Kid was about to light the fuse. "Enough palavering!" His voice had gone shrill. "I got me a hankering to get better acquainted with my little sister and that pretty lawyer. Send all four of them out. I'll give you five minutes. Then we put a match to your so-called courthouse!"

Stark didn't wait to hear any more. He had to move fast if he was to have any chance of bulldogging the Kid. And he didn't really have much chance at all. He needed position and firepower. In order to give Prudence and the rest a chance to escape, he must scatter the Kid's forces. One man against a small army of gunsels. Not good odds.

He loped back to Red and swung into the saddle. At a gallop, he put the big sorrel down the rutted street, slewing him around a corner and then into an alley running behind most of the businesses on one side of Main Street. He reined to a halt and sprang to the ground.

A lot of firepower . . . He hesitated, then pulled the Evans old-model repeater from the scabbard he'd rigged for it. Just now, he'd favor the Evans, with its thirty-four loads, over either of his usual saddle guns.

A rickety staircase gave access to the second story, and from the landing there he pulled himself up onto the flat roof. Mentally he was counting the minutes and seconds. Both were getting away from him.

The Sooner Kid's lewd threat against Prudence and the other women was still ringing in Stark's ears. More than ever now, he considered his battle against the Kid to be a personal one.

As he reached the parapet at the edge of the roof, gunfire rolled up from the street. Dropping to one knee, he peered over. He was almost directly across the street from the courthouse. Several of the riflemen had started throwing lead to keep the occupants pinned down. The rifle fire was obviously to cover one hombre who was edging his horse closer to the building. As Stark watched, a lighted torch flared into life in the man's hand.

Stark's eyebrows drew down in a scowl. He'd wanted to try picking off the Sooner Kid with his first shot. Once the outlaw leader was dead, the others likely would've scattered, defusing the powderkeg. But now he reckoned he didn't have that option. He worked the S-shaped lever of the Evans, set the sights on the would-be arsonist, and squeezed the trigger.

At this range it was an easy shot, and for a moment the report of the Evans was lost in the roll of gunfire from the mounted men in the street. Then the torch bearer rocked backward and toppled out of his saddle. As he fell to the ground, the torch brushed his skittish mount, and the beast arched its back and sunfished wildly.

Stark shifted his attention swiftly, trying to get the Kid in his sights, but the outlaw was too quick on the uptake. He glimpsed the falling rider and instantly ducked low over his saddle, his long hair flying out behind him like a greasy halo. Stark's shot sailed past him to scar the boardwalk in front of the courthouse.

Once the mob of horsemen realized they'd come under fire, they went wild, shouting, cursing, and sending bullets flying in every direction. To Stark's dismay, the Kid was quickly lost in the resulting furor. All he could do was concentrate on the remaining outlaws. He levered and fired; levered and fired, trying to drop a man with each shot.

He missed some of his targets, but he hit most. A horseman flung up his arms and lurched backward into the melee of dust and milling hooves. Another reeled in his saddle, but managed to hold on as his horse broke free of the confusion and bolted away up the street.

Stark shifted aim and fired, shifted aim again, sometimes not even waiting to see if his target fell. Smoke wreathed his face and he blinked his eyes to clear them of powder smoke, mentally ticking off the bullets as he used them. He'd completely lost track of the Sooner Kid. At least one horse was down—the result of a wild shot by one of the gunmen, he guessed. He hadn't targeted any of the milling, bucking beasts.

A bullet chipped the heavy board of the parapet. Someone had spotted him. He ducked low and scrambled a few feet to the side, clear of the smoke. Rising up, he opened fire again. The hombre who'd snapped a shot at him spun and fell, the six-shooter flying from his hand. Not bad shooting for a handgun, Stark registered grudgingly.

The mob was breaking up beneath his relentless rifle fire. Riderless horses streaked away from the uproar for the open prairie. Riders fought the remaining mounts to regain control, then spurred them in that same direction. Men on foot raced for cover, firing wildly.

The Evans was hot—almost scorching—in Stark's grip. He was breathing harshly and his ears rang like the inside of a bell. His shoulder throbbed from the big rifle's recoil. His targets were scattering like quail under a diving hawk. He only had two more shots left, if he'd counted correctly. He couldn't even venture a guess at how few seconds it had taken him to empty the Evans . . . or how many bodies now lay sprawled lifelessly in the street. And he didn't have time to start counting corpses.

The door to the saloon *cum* courthouse suddenly burst open, and a burly figure came crashing out like a grizzly charging from its den. In one big fist Judge Horatio Hatch wielded the pistol grip sawed-off as easily as another man would fire a six-gun. It belched flame and thunder, his arm barely twitching at the recoil. Two gunmen were knocked kicking. Hatch's shaggy head swiveled on his bull neck, and he snapped a shot from the revolver in his other hand. Stark couldn't see where the bullet went, but he heard a man scream in response.

Just then the dark slender form of Thaddeus Jenkins slipped out of the courthouse in the judge's wake. From a duelist's stance the bailiff sighted down the long barrel of his handgun and picked off a hardcase who was leveling his pistol at Hatch's ample back.

Stark knew the battlefront had now moved to street level, and he wanted in on the action. He kicked the last two shots out of the Evans and set it aside. It had done him yeomen's service. He dashed across the roof and dropped down to the landing, taking the stairs two at a time after that. Pausing to snatch the repeating shotgun from the saddle of the snorting Red, he dashed around the corner of the building to take up the fray anew.

There was still the Sooner Kid to be dealt with.

Chapter Thirteen

The street had been cleared for the moment. Judge Hatch swung about at the sound of Stark's footfalls. He let out an expressive grunt of recognition.

"Figured that was you, Peacemaker. Obliged. You saved our bacon. Couldn't get off a shot for them yahoos throwing lead through the windows."

Thaddeus paced forward, reloading his pistol as he moved. His eyes scanned the street and the buildings lining it. He spared Stark a tight nod and a small grin.

William Fuller appeared in the doorway of the courthouse, a rifle gripped in his fists. There was a flutter of movement at his back, and Prudence slipped past him. She paused on the boardwalk, knowing better than to come into the open just yet. Stark reached her in three long-legged strides.

"All of us are fine," she greeted him breathlessly. Then she added, "You were right. He was planning to kill us."

"Maybe half right," Stark allowed. "I didn't figure him to come back here so fast, or with so many men."

Prudence's full lips parted slightly as though words trembled there to be spoken.

"Let's go run these varmints out of my town!" Hatch burst out. "Fuller here can stay and protect the womenfolk. He ain't in any shape to go gallavanting around none."

"We can do a little protecting of ourselves now that you've cleared the pass," Sarah Dunsmore spoke up from just inside the courthouse. She was hefting a rifle herself. "Clarence Dunsmore didn't figure a woman had any place on the frontier unless she could sight down a barrel and pull a trigger."

Donna had eased forward to shadow her fiance. She was also armed.

"We'll be all right now, Jim. Go ahead," Prudence urged.

"Guess I'm back to taking orders," Stark said so softly only she could hear, and winked. Wheeling to Hatch and Thaddeus he jacked a shell into the chamber of the shotgun. "You heard the lady. Let's clear the town."

They spread out to work the street. Stark in the middle, the judge and his bailiff each taking one side of the avenue. Glancing back, Stark saw the women disappearing into the courthouse. Fuller remained just inside the doorway watching for signs of trouble.

For the moment there was none. Stark's position in the center of the street was a mixed blessing. He had a better view of the buildings and cross streets, but he also made a better target.

Warily they advanced, sweeping the street with practiced, watchful eyes. Hatch still toted his shotgun. He'd stuck his pistol under his belt and looked to be enjoying himself. Thaddeus, likewise, carried an extra iron. He paced forward with studied deliberation. No townsfolk risked showing themselves.

From the edge of his vision, Stark glimpsed movement in a window as Thaddeus passed below. He saw a whiskered face above a pointing six-gun. Swiveling, he fired from the hip. The blast of Hatch's shotgun mingled with the tail end of his own weapon's report. The window, part of the wall surrounding it, and the ambusher all disappeared as if struck by a giant fist.

Unperturbed, Thaddeus gave a calm nod of appreciation.

"I had him," Stark advised Hatch dryly.

"I was afraid you'd miss."

One side of Stark's mouth quirked upwards. He thumbed a replacement load from his bandolier into the shotgun. From somewhere he heard the fading sound of horse's hooves. One of the Kid's hardcases hightailing it, he figured.

There was another one who wasn't. He stepped from behind the corner of a building, lifting a rifle to his shoulder. Thaddeus's black-sleeved arm snapped out straight. He fired twice. The rifleman's weapon tilted and blasted the sky. He fell backwards out of sight.

"Took you two shots," the judge commented.

"Nerves, Your Honor," Thaddeus said coolly.

Hatch snorted. The rifleman lay motionless as they passed.

The edge of town was some hundred yards ahead of them. Looking back, Stark saw they'd covered several blocks. Reins trailing, a riderless horse trotted across the street ahead of them and was almost ventilated by two shotguns and a pistol. Stark grimaced in disgust. Nerves, sure enough. Glancing around, he saw all was clear. How many of the Kid's pack were left? he wondered.

Some seventy-five yards in front of them, several horsemen suddenly roiled into the street, filling it. The Kid had regained control of some of his forces, Stark realized. He was fixing to mount a charge.

Stark and his companions came to a halt.

"I'll cover you if you miss, Your Honor," Stark said.

Hatch let out a choked grunt of laughter, then said, "You do that. Here they come!"

And come they did, spurring their horses, yelling, and shooting. Some of them fired wild, others with more purpose. Hatch and his bailiff drew their extra handguns. Stark lifted his shotgun to his shoulder. The riders came like a wave cresting on a river. Stark felt the vibrations beneath his feet. A bullet whizzed past his head.

"Reckon now's the time," he said.

To have fled before a mounted charge would've been disaster. This might be, too, but it took determined riders to charge straight into the maw of concentrated firepower.

Stark and his companions opened fire in the same instant. The shotgun kicked his shoulder almost before he himself knew he'd fired. He worked right to left, buckshot loads alternating with the thumb-sized slugs. He was aware of Thaddeus on his left alternating fire with a six-gun in each hand, and the judge, both arms extended, cutting loose with shotgun and pistol. Stark levered and fired, levered and fired.

Horses and men alike went down beneath that withering fusillade. Through a haze of powdersmoke Stark saw the carnage. His shotgun was dry. Dropping it, he swiped the .45 Peacemaker from its holster and began to snap shots at the still-oncoming mass of gunflashes, men, and horseflesh. Dust raised by the onslaught merged with the smoke from his gun and that of his companions.

Fifty feet from them, the charge broke. Men slewed their horses aside or dived headlong from their saddles in a jumble of confusion. The whole affair had taken only a matter of seconds. One horse without a rider charged on past between Stark and Thaddeus. He glimpsed one of its wildly rolling eyes as it thundered by.

"Smoke them out!" Hatch bellowed. He lumbered forward, fumbling shells from a coatpocket to reload the sawed-off.

They separated into the sidestreeets. Stark prowled warily. After the crash and roar of gunfire, the avenues and alleys were eerily silent, occupied, it seemed only by shadows. He'd seen the kid in the midst of the charge, then lost track of him. Where was he lurking now? Then one shadow took the form of a man and Stark wheeled sharply, ratcheting the shotgun. "Freeze!"

Caught with his iron half-lifted, the hombre became like a statue.

"Drop it!" Stark ordered.

The six-gun hit the dirt. The man's eyes were wide. His features didn't register with Stark. "Slope, or you're coyote bait!" he growled.

The fellow turned and bolted like a rabbit.

Stark eased up, then ducked instinctively as he heard a repeater being levered to full cock.

A shot tore the air above him. He had a fragment's view of a rifle barrel being hastily withdrawn behind the corner of a building. Straightening, in a single movement, he brought up the shotgun and fired. The solid load punched through both sides of the building's corner, and a man cried out sharply. A rifle fell into view.

Stark rushed forward, firing a load of buckshot as he charged. Rounding the building's corner, he found himself sighting down the barrel of the shotgun at Nash's sprawled form. The Kid's segundo was no longer dapper. Both the slug and some of the buckshot had caught him.

He stared up at Stark and recognized him. "Had to be you," he said bitterly.

"Had to be somebody," Stark agreed. He let the shotgun dangle in his left hand.

"Go to the devil, Peacemaker." Nash coughed.

"Not likely. But I reckon you're fixing to meet him."

Nash shuddered and went limp.

Stark pushed air out of his lungs. Now that Nash was busy meeting his new boss, that left only—

"Fill your hand, Peacemaker!"

It was the Kid's voice, and he was directly to Stark's left, already hauling iron in a cross-draw. He'd been set up,

Stark realized, just like William Fuller. He should've expected it, but there was no time to berate himself for being a fool, no time to even turn toward the Kid to defend himself. There was only time to draw and fire across his own body.

It was an awkward shot, a draw slower than his best, but it drilled the Sooner Kid dead center just as the Kid's gun fired. Stark heard that bullet whipcrack past. He pivoted full about and triggered again to make sure the Kid didn't get off a second shot.

He cocked the Peacemaker a third time. Smoke trailing from its barrel, he walked deliberately over to where the Kid lay spreadeagled on his back. He kicked the Kid's fallen gun spinning away across the dirt and out of reach. But the Kid was almost finished. It showed in the rapidly growing paleness of his dissolute features.

"Tucker saw you draw," he managed to croak the words up at Stark. "He swore I could beat you."

"Tucker's a fool," Stark replied flatly. "He saw me kill a two-bit gunman I knew I could beat. I didn't have to try very hard. With you it was different. I didn't take any chances. I tried a mite harder."

The Kid snarled in frustration, and the light went out of his eyes.

A flurry of shots sounded elsewhere in the town. Thaddeus and Hatch doing some mopping up, Stark reckoned. For himself, he figured this fight was over.

"Well, Peacemaker, if Thaddeus here ever quits me, I'll sure enough track you down and hire you to be my bailiff. I think you could keep order nigh as well as he can."

Solemnly Stark shook his head. "No thanks, Your Honor. Your courtroom's too rough for me. I'll stick to trouble-shooting. It's a lot more tame."

Hatch chuckled, and behind him, Thaddeus grinned.

Hatch waved a bottle dwarfed in his big fist. "Sure you won't have some of this here champagne? Best in town. Come to think of it, likely the only champagne in town." He laughed at his own joke.

"No, thanks. That's too strong for me, too," Stark demurred.

Hatch shook his shaggy head. "You and Miss McKay have just got too much temperance in you. That being the case, I'll go check on the other guests." He lumbered off across the courtroom where Prudence was in close conversation with the Dunsmore women and William Fuller.

What had started out as a brief probate hearing had rapidly evolved into a kind of celebration with Hatch producing two bottles of champagne and shot glasses from under the bar, then proceeding to serve as bartender between healthy swigs from one of the bottles. Apparently, judicial impartiality in the case had gone by the wayside, although he still wore his black robe.

Stark cocked an eyebrow at Thaddeus. "If you ever need a hand riding herd on that overgrown bearcat, don't come asking me for help," he drawled.

The bailiff laughed quietly. "Just so I don't have to try and restore the order the next time you're involved in a case, I'll be satisfied. But I'm mighty glad you got up on the roof with that Evans repeater before matters went any further. It sounded like an army up there, rather than a mighty good man with a mighty good rifle."

"The rifle's yours if you want it," Stark offered. "I've got enough firepower to tote around already. And like you say, a good rifle should belong to a good man."

Thaddeus nodded his acceptance. "I am beholden to you."

"Just look after the judge, and keep him out of trouble."

Thaddeus grinned and chuckled. "That's a powerful order, but I'll do my best."

Stark saw Prudence leave her clients and come toward him. Thaddeus took note of her approach as well.

"I'll leave you two to be alone," he said, and moved away.

Folks always seemed to be doing that when it came to him and Prudence, Stark reflected. But this time that was all right. It fit into his plan.

There was a lightness to Prudence's step. She was almost as bubbly as the champagne. "We did it!" she beamed. "The rest of the probate proceedings will only be formalities. And I've just learned that William and Donna are going to be married. William will stay out here and help run the ranch. They've asked Judge Hatch to perform the ceremony before they leave to go home, and we're invited."

He and Prudence got invited to a lot of weddings, too, Stark noted. Which was also all right.

Prudence suddenly grew more serious. "I came over here for a reason. I need to thank you for doing all you did to protect us, and for—for being a gentleman when we were alone together on the trail."

"That wasn't hard. With a lady, there wasn't any choice."

Prudence flushed at his words, then looked earnestly up at him. "You look a little troubled still," she said with a small frown. "Is something going on that I'm not aware of?"

Stark cleared his throat. "There is something that I need to talk to you about. Care to go for a walk?"

She glanced nervously about at the other celebrants. "Should we tell someone where we're going?"

"No need. There's no trouble brewing, and we won't be gone long."

"No trouble, huh?" Suspicion replaced the nervousness in Prudence's voice. "Then what are you up to?"

"Never mind," Stark said irritably. "For once, just don't ask so many questions."

Prudence shrugged and allowed him to compel her out of the back door. Behind the building the prairie stretched away to the horizon. Stark set a slow pace toward an ancient cottonwood tree a few yards off.

Prudence ventured a provocative smile. "So what did you want to talk about?"

"Well, these past few days have set me to thinking about where my life was heading. And for the first time ever, I began to feeling that maybe something was missing."

"Oh? And what might that something be?"

He paused under the shade from the tree and turned toward her. "You," he said simply.

"Me?" She looked ready to laugh, then sobered as she grasped his meaning. "You mean . . . marriage?" She sounded almost frightened.

Stark gathered his courage and pressed on. "Are you saying you never thought along those lines?"

She hesitated, then an honesty came into her eyes. "All right. I'll admit I *hoped* that marriage might enter the picture for us at some point. But I thought it would be sometime in the future."

"Yeah, me, too." Stark shoved his fists nervously into his pockets. "I figured on down the road a piece, we might—" He pulled his thoughts up short and got back on the trail. "But out there on the prairie, in that tent, with you lying beside me. . . . It just felt so natural . . . and so right. Then when I rode into town and saw that the Sooner Kid had you and the others pinned down in the courthouse . . . Well, since then I've been thinking the future's not all that certain for any of us—"

"And maybe we shouldn't wait?" Prudence broke in. "I must confess that when I was crouched behind that bar with all those bullets flying in and there seemed no hope against such overwhelming odds, my one regret was that we hadn't—" She stopped abruptly as her cheeks stained red. Then she hurriedly finished, "That we hadn't gotten to know each other any better than we had."

"Yeah." Stark smiled knowingly. "So should I tell Judge Hatch he can plan on a double wedding when he marries William and Donna?"

She looked up at him as though he'd lost his mind. "Not on your life! We're getting married in a church, not a saloon. And I need time to plan our wedding. My father will want to come and give me away, and I'll have to shop for an appropriate wedding gown. Since I was a little girl, I've dreamed of being married in a long white dress—"

"Now, hold on," Stark interrupted teasingly. "I don't know if you're entitled to wear white after that night we spent alone together in that tent unchaperoned."

"But nothing happened!" Prudence exclaimed.

"Yeah, you know that. And I know that. But nobody's gonna believe it when they hear the circumstances."

"Jim Stark! You're not saying you'll spread false rumors?"

"I might, if these wedding plans of yours get too outta hand. I'm not about to get dressed up in no monkey suit."

She laughed and reached up to circle her arms about his neck. "Okay. You win. We'll both wear our nicest church clothes and invite only our closest family and friends."

"That's better." He put his hands on her trim waist and drew her closer to plant a long lingering kiss on her upturned lips. "I'm glad you decided to be reasonable," he said as the kiss ended. "I was mighty worried about my reputation. If word got out about your loose behavior, I'd be seriously compromised—"

"Oh, you're incorrigible! And I take it back! You're no gentleman!" Prudence cried as she stepped away from him and slapped his shoulder stingingly.

"Ow!" Stark pressed a hand to the spot. "Now I need another of those massages you're so good at. And maybe a shave."

"I don't believe it would be a good idea to let me close to you with a razor just now."

"I'll keep that in mind." After a span of seconds, Stark

realized they were both standing motionless, staring fool-ishly at one another.

Or maybe it wasn't so foolish. He lowered his lips to hers again for a final kiss before they headed back. She seemed as reluctant as he was to bring the embrace to an end, but they'd been gone long enough. The others would be getting curious about their whereabouts.

Stark was feeling oddly content as he took Prudence's hand and started back toward the building. It had been a good day. He'd stopped a hired killer and a ruthless gun-man from ever killing again. He'd broken up a brutal out-law gang. He'd helped protect a family of decent and honest folks.

And he had the respect—and love—of a beautiful and virtuous woman. A woman who had now agreed to be his wife.

Maybe his legacy wasn't looking so bad after all.

Epilogue

James Stark stood nervously in the anteroom off the altar at the front of the church. Through a crack in the door he peered out at the beribboned and flower-filled sanctuary that was rapidly filling with people.

So much for a small wedding, he thought wryly.

But he had to admit it wasn't altogether Prudence's fault that things had gotten so out of hand. Once word got around the territory that he and the lady lawyer were planning to tie the knot, seems like everyone they encountered wanted an invite to the festivities. And Prudence couldn't seem to find the words to turn them down.

When he had protested, she had thrown up her hands and given that responsibility over to him. And to his consternation, he'd discovered he wasn't any better at it than she was.

He found that he, maybe more than Prudence, had too many ties to too many people—people who were surprisingly grateful for the help and protection of a troubleshooter named the Peacemaker who'd intervened in their lives over the years. Some of the incidents these well-wishers had related to him he didn't even remember. They'd merely been by-products of him pursuing some case or other. But they'd changed people's lives—and always, it seemed, for the better.

He heard the door open behind him, and he turned to find that Prudence had entered the room already dressed in her wedding attire. He quickly closed the door to the sanctuary and stood leaning against it.

He managed a scowl in spite of the pleasure that welled up in him at the sight of her. "Should you even be here? I mean, isn't it against the rules or something for the groom to see the bride right before the wedding?"

She laughed. "That's all superstition. It's supposed to be bad luck for you to see me in my wedding dress before the ceremony or something. But since neither of us is superstitious, and since I've already modeled the dress for you, that doesn't really apply to us, does it?"

"I guess not," he allowed. Seeing her in that dress a few weeks ago had been another reason he'd relented on having a big wedding. She'd dragged him into a fancy dress shop to show it to him. And after he saw her in it, he couldn't deny her the chance to look that beautiful on the most important day of their lives. She'd looked like a true vision in the silk brocade concoction.

She looked even more beautiful today—more radiant

somehow. The dress wasn't frilly at all. Frills wouldn't have been right for her. It was more tailored and form-fitting, with a panel down the back that barely trailed on the floor.

She hadn't wanted a veil either, which suited him fine. He could just see himself getting all tangled up trying to fold the fool thing back away from her face, like he'd seen done in other weddings he'd attended. Prudence's choice of a pert little hat with ribbons hanging down in the back had been the right touch.

And the smile she wore now as she gazed at him was the best part of the whole getup. It took his breath away.

"You never did tell me why you're here," he teased. "The preacher showed me where you were dressing right before he stuck me in this room to wait. And your room is all the way at the back of the church."

She laughed again. "I know. But I had to come check on you. I was afraid you'd get cold feet and run out on me. I couldn't bear the thought of getting left at the altar."

"No chance." He crossed the room to take her in his arms. "You're stuck with me . . . permanent. Especially after today." He bent to kiss her lightly on the lips. "I must admit, though, I'd rather face a nest of owlhoots than walk into that sanctuary and face all those people out there. Can you imagine the ribbing I'll get if I trip, or drop the ring, or step on your foot or something? I'm completely out of my element, you know."

"Yes, I know." She reached up and pecked him on the cheek. "You're much more at home waiting to waylay some bank robber than waiting for me to traipse down the aisle." Her tone changed subtly then. "But the reward, though different, can be just as gratifying. Remember, the honeymoon's only hours away."

"Hey, I'm well aware of that," he said huskily. "But why don't we speed things up a bit? I'll go grab that preacher. He can marry us in here, and we'll sneak out the back way and get on with our lives."

She pushed against him and pretended outrage. "And disappoint all our friends and relatives? My father is looking forward to giving me away. He never thought he'd get rid of me."

"Then he'll appreciate us speeding up the process. What do you say? Want to make a break for it?"

"Jim!" She slapped him on the arm. "This is our wedding—not a jailbreak!"

He grinned down on her. "Had you going for a minute, didn't I? Still, I've never been more nervous in my life."

"But you'll make it. I have every confidence in you. Besides, if that crowd out there gives you any trouble, you can pull a gun on them."

"No, I can't. That preacher took my gunbelt."

She slid her arms around his waist and made a great show of feeling for his hideout gun. "What? No .38 in your waistband?"

"What can I say? That preacher takes a firm stand against gunplay at the weddings he performs."

She laughed out loud. "Will you cut it out? I know the preacher had no part in your decision to come unarmed."

He shrugged. "You're right. The new suit didn't fit right over a gunbelt. And I had to do my best to measure up to you today. Didn't want folks to think you'd married beneath your station."

"No chance of that." The warm glow in her eyes made him catch his breath. "Everyone here knows I'm marrying the most wonderful man in the world."

Clever words escaped him this time. He folded her into his arms and held her tightly for a moment before thrusting her toward the door. "Hey, you'd better get out of here."

She nodded. "Yeah. I'll see you out there in a few minutes."

Stark watched her go with a lump in his throat. He turned and opened the door to the sanctuary again, watching for his cue on when to enter and get this show on the road.

There were more people than ever now, and the organ had begun to play soft background music. He'd asked Marshal Nix to be his best man, and he knew the lawman was waiting at the back of the church to escort Prudence's maid of honor—some cousin or other—down the aisle. Yes, he, Stark, was only minutes away from becoming a married man.

And he had no regrets. He'd never been happier.

He let his eyes roam over the sea of faces in the church auditorium, all looking expectant and happy . . . for him.

He thought again about his legacy—the important things he'd leave behind him at the end of his life. They were many and positive, he decided, and growing in number every day.

Some days more than others. And this was one of those days.

The preacher suddenly made an entrance from the anteroom opposite the one Stark was in. He nodded, and Stark stepped out to stand in front of him, as they'd practiced the night before. Then both of them turned to face the back of the church as Nix and Prudence's attendant walked in solemnly. Following that Prudence and her father appeared in the doorway.

The organ music swelled into the traditional wedding march, and the lump in Stark's throat swelled with it. Prudence's eyes met his and held them, never wavering as she floated down the aisle toward him.

He knew he was too nervous to remember much else of what took place today, but the look on her face would be forever etched in his memory. It was hard to believe he could be loved that deeply by such a talented and desirable woman.

But he was. It was all there in her eyes and in the smile that wreathed her lovely face.

All at once he knew the good things happening in his life weren't over yet. Not by a long shot.